Anne Manning

Meadowleigh

A tale of English country life. Vol. 2

Anne Manning

Meadowleigh
A tale of English country life. Vol. 2

ISBN/EAN: 9783337174620

Printed in Europe, USA, Canada, Australia, Japan

Cover: Foto ©Andreas Hilbeck / pixelio.de

More available books at **www.hansebooks.com**

MEADOWLEIGH.

MEADOWLEIGH:

A TALE OF ENGLISH COUNTRY LIFE.

BY THE

AUTHOR OF "THE LADIES OF BEVER HOLLOW."

"Give me again my hollow tree,
My crust of bread and liberty!"

IN TWO VOLUMES.

VOL. II.

LONDON:

RICHARD BENTLEY, NEW BURLINGTON STREET.

1863.

LONDON :
Printed by A. Schulze, 13, Poland Street.

MEADOWLEIGH.

CHAPTER I.

There, at her chamber-window high,
A lonely maiden sits;
Its casement fronts the western sky,
And balmy air admits.

Is it to watch the setting sun
She does that seat prefer?
Alas! the maiden thinks of one
Who never thinks of her.

ELEANOR sat at her bed-room window with her letter in her hand, looking sadly out on the undulating common, and the longer she looked, the sadder she grew. It was only some grief, loss, or pain that had been, thou-

B

sands of times before, and would be again,
but to her it was as sharp and bitter as if
made for herself alone.   It saddened all nature—it deadened hope.

Yet did she not lament with loud allew
As women wont, but with deep sighs, and singulfs few.

After all, how sharp are the trials of the
young! We make light of them afterwards,
but only because they are lessened by distance.
Besides, the sorrows of the young have
often a dignity which those of the elderly
want; they are mainly sorrows of the affec-
tions, not of disappointed ambition or pe-
cuniary expectations.   The idol of seeming
gold has turned out to be of clay; *that* is a
very frequent grief indeed! sometimes a lover,
or one that we had hoped might become a
lover, sometimes a bosom friend.

These are respectable grievances, my young
friends; only, all the tears in the world won't
remedy them!   They are to do you good in

one way or another. Think how much hammering the polished steel requires. Through
how many waters the Australian diggers rinse
their gold! How long the wood, of which
musical instruments are made, takes to
season before it will *stand!* Do not we then,
need much hammering, much sifting, much
seasoning?

Ashamed, at length, of remaining so long
alone with her sorrow, Eleanor went down
stairs, and found Miss Clairvaux immersed in
the perusal of a small, old-looking book.
She sat down to work in a listless way.

"Eleanor," said Miss Clairvaux presently,
" did you ever read De la Rochefoucault's
Maxims?"

" No," said Eleanor in surprise, "is he not
very cynical and unsafe?"

"Unsafe to those who do not know how
to take him, perhaps," said Miss Clairvaux,
" but deeply versed in the natural heart,
before it knows God. And some of his pre-

cepts are of universal application. How true, now, this is, 'Weakness is the only defect of the mind that cannot be amended.' "

" Yes," said Eleanor, beginning to consider a little. " Perhaps it is so. But how disheartening !"

" Here is something to qualify it. 'We have more power than will. And 'tis often to excuse ourselves to ourselves that we fancy things impossible to be effected."

" Does that improve the matter ?"

" Certainly it *may*. I, for instance, may despond and think I am too weak for some given effort."

" You ?"

" *Par exemple*. But then I think, 'nay, I have the power, 'tis only the will is wanting.' I try and find I have the power."

" Just so," said Eleanor, absently.

" Here again," pursued Miss Clairvaux. " ' There is no accident so unfortunate, but the prudent will draw some advantage from it.' "

"Dear Miss Clairvaux, do you think that is true?"

"I am persuaded of it, Eleanor! Here again—" she resumed presently, "'Flattery is a false coin, which would have no currency but for our vanity.'"

"That's *very* good," said Eleanor. Miss Clairvaux was silent for some time, but at length read out the following, with strong approval.

"''Tis more dishonourable to distrust our friends than to be deceived by them.'"

"Is it?" said Eleanor, quickly. "Oh, that is a comforting saying!"

"I think it quite true," said Miss Clairvaux. "It is very bitter to find we have been deceived by our friends; but it reflects no discredit on us—which it does to distrust them."

"If they *ought* to be distrusted—"

"Yes, supposing them artful enough to mask their faithlessness. One grows very unamiable if one is always suspecting."

They talked in this way till Eleanor became calmer. Yet though her trouble showed itself less on the surface, her former cheerfulness was gone. Miss Clairvaux noted day by day her pale cheeks, heavy eyes, and faded appetite. Impatient of leaving any evil unremedied which it was in her power at least to mitigate, she said one morning:

"Eleanor, would you like to go home?"

"Oh! so much!" exclaimed Eleanor. "I hope you do not think me ungrateful!"

"I have no such nonsensical thoughts. It is quite simple that you should like to see your mother; and that she should like to see you."

Eleanor gratefully kissed her, and then said:

"How long may I stay?"

"As long as you like, my love! You have no real tie here."

"Oh, Miss Clairvaux! not the tie of affection?"

"Ah, that tie does not always hold! But, in our case it will—I have no fears."

"You *need* have none of me. I shall love you all the better for this goodness."

"Pray do not use so fine a word. You have contributed to my happiness more than I have to yours."

Eleanor smiled and shook her head. "I do not think it."

After a short pause, "And may I really come back again?" said she.

"My dear, how can you doubt it? I shall look for your return with lively pleasure. There is no luxury I should be so sorry to deny myself. Nay, you are more than a luxury, you are a safeguard. Think how fearful my position would have been, with Mr. Foljambe in the house, and you out of it!"

"Perhaps I had better not go," said Eleanor, doubtfully.

"On *his* account? oh, we shall see no

more of him. He only looks in, about once in seven years—quite often enough! You gave him such a fright that he will not hastily repeat the experiment; and how should he know of your absence?"

"Well, I am glad you think there is no danger of it," said Eleanor, "or else I could not enjoy the treat you have offered me."

That she did enjoy the prospect of it was unmistakeably shown in her altered voice, look, and manner. It gave Miss Clairvaux a pang; yet she chid herself for feeling it.

"I am nothing to her; and her mother everything. What can be more natural? more reasonable? I, the friend of a few months—so much her senior—I may well be surprised and thankful that she loves me as much as she does."

Yet she felt a little upset by it, nevertheless; could hardly help being a little cross.

Eleanor was to write word of her coming

by the evening post, and start on her journey the following morning.

"How glad George will be!" said she.

Talk of a person and he appears. Five minutes afterwards, George walked in, with a broad smile on his face, as if secure of a welcome.

"Well, to be sure!" cried Miss Clairvaux, looking up and seeing him. "Who would have thought of seeing you, Mr. George?"

"I hope I don't intrude, ma'am?" said he smartly.

"Is anything the matter?"

"O dear, no! The whim seized me that I should like to see Nelly, and I didn't think you would be altogether sorry to see me— so here I am."

"All my beds were slept in last night," said Miss Clairvaux, coldly. Eleanor changed colour at the altered tone. George looked rather blank.

"Of course, ma'am, I can sleep at the

inn," said he, more quietly, "or, indeed, I can go back to-night if you don't wish to have me."

"Who said I did not wish to have you? And *the* inn? when we have several? A likely thing I should send you to one of them, when my beds were only slept in last night to keep them aired."

"Oh, all's right, then," said George, relieved, as he saw her pleasant smile beginning to play at the corners of her lips. "You really frightened me, ma'am, for I thought I had come at an unpropitious moment."

And she had frightened Eleanor, too.

"You came at a moment when I felt desperately cross, at the prospect of parting with this dear girl."

"With Eleanor?" exclaimed he.

"Yes, I was going to send her home to see her mother."

"Why, then I can take her! How lucky it was that I came!"

" Well," said Miss Clairvaux laughing, " you may choose to say so, but you might have saved your money, for you know you did not come to see *me*."

" In a secondary way, ma'am," said George.

"Oh," she replied gaily, "how do you know I shall not be affronted at being put second ?"

" Well, somehow, ma'am, I seem to feel I *do* know it," and the dialogue went on in the same strain, immensely relieving Eleanor by the perfect good understanding between them, which, for a moment, George seemed to have endangered.

Afterwards, Miss Clairvaux said :

" Old Sir John More, father of Sir Thomas, used to be fond of comparing women to a bagfull of snakes ; saying, that if you put you hand in and chanced to find an eel, you might think yourself lucky. I almost think I am as slippery as an eel sometimes—people don't know where to have me. For, you see, George, I never let people take liberties ; and, directly they think they have me in their own hands, I turn round upon them."

"And a very good way too, ma'am," said George. "Teaches fellows not to reckon on your spare bed!"

She laughed; and Eleanor wondered how they could say such things, and was relieved when the conversation turned.

George brought a letter from his mother to Eleanor, on the Foljambe affair, which, having hastily run through, she gave to Miss Clair-vaux, who, after glancing at it, said:

"If you can spare me this letter, Eleanor, I shall be glad to read it quietly when I am alone. Thank you—thank you. Do *you* know anythiug of this business, Mr. Gray-don?"

"Not a word, ma'am," said George, stolidly.

"All the better. I will dismiss it from

my thoughts at present; and enjoy your company while I can."

George had many droll, and some affecting stories to relate, and the evening flew away with unwonted swiftness. After they had separated for the night, Miss Clairvaux gave Mrs. Graydon's letter an attentive perusal. She had been unavoidably delayed in writing it. It was very sympathetic and comforting; and expressed strong opinions in regard to Mr. Foljambe. Miss Clairvaux did not retire to rest till she had written a cordial note to Mrs. Graydon, expressing sentiments towards Eleanor which would inevitably gladden her heart. Even then, though it was getting rather late (as people counted lateness at the Peaked House), she tapped at Eleanor's door, and found her packing her box.

"My dear Eleanor," said she, "your quarter is within a few days of being up, and here is your salary."

"Dear Miss Ciairvaux, 1 can wait till I return—"

"No, no, delays are dangerous. I shall be in your debt then. Always take money that belongs to you when it is offered. I wish it were more, my dear."

And she gave her a long kiss.

"You are a great comfort to me, Eleanor."

Eleanor was touched, and returned her embrace warmly, without speaking. She lay awake afterwards, thinking of her with a wistful pity, for being so isolated. Her own inclinations were all social. As for the money, it certainly was acceptable enough.

In consequence of George's arrival, Eleanor's letter to her mother had been given up; it would be such a delightful surprise to her to see both her children return home together. They started the following morning, and a tear shone in Miss Clairvaux's eye as she returned Eleanor's parting kiss. Having watched them out of sight, she turned to her usual avocations, and was sensible of a blank in the house; but by dinner-time the feeling of dullness had worn off, for persons accustomed to solitude are apt to prefer their own company even to that of the best companions in the world; not from any unsociality, but love of freedom, of stillness, and of rest.

Meanwhile the brother and sister sped to London with railway swiftness, and soon found themselves in an omnibus, traversing the long space between Paddington and Riadore Place. The little house was unambitious enough, with a little strip of grass-plat and mean iron railing dividing it from the Camberwell Road, yet to Eleanor it was the most beloved spot on earth, for it held her mother. Soon they were in one another's arms, and Mrs. Graydon was as surprised and delighted as they had anticipated, nor did she immediately perceive anything amiss in Eleanor's looks. They all three talked rapidly and joyously for a little while, and then George went off to the hospital, and the mother and daughter were left together. Mrs. Graydon then said, "you do not look as well, Elly, as you did. What is the matter?"

"Oh nothing particular," faltered Eleanor.

"Come! out with it," said her mother, kissing her. "Surely, you and Miss Clairvaux have had no misunderstanding?"

"O no, indeed, mamma! She is as kind as can be. O no, it was only a tiresome, disappointing letter I had from Sophy Day. I don't know what right I had to be disappointed about it, either."

"About what?"

"Maurice is going to be —— you can read it if you like," said Eleanor, faltering.

Mrs. Graydon hastily ran through the letter, and then exclaimed, "I don't believe one word of it!"

"O, mamma! don't you?"

"Not one word! It's just like Sophy. And not a bit like Maurice. Don't distrust him, Eleanor! He'll be true to you, you'll see, if you have but faith and patience."

"I am sure I am very willing to have faith and patience," said Eleanor, feeling immensely relieved. "Only, she seems so positive —"

"Let her be positive or superlative," said Mrs. Graydon. "*I* have confidence in him, and why should not you?"

CHAPTER II.

Fer.—Where should this music be? i' the air, or the
    earth?

THE sweet feeling of hope, restored by her
mother's confident assertions, brought back
the bloom to Eleanor's cheeks which country
breezes had been unable to maintain. A
light heart makes a merry countenance; and
oh! how glad the young are to believe what
they wish!

It was a happy little home now, and
Eleanor failed not to write cheerful and
grateful letters to Miss Clairvaux. To her

surprise, not one of these letters was answered; and this was the more remarkable, because Miss Clairvaux was not only fond of writing, but had very strong opinions about not leaving letters unanswered. Could she have taken umbrage at anything? Could she be ill?"

"I wish she may not have some new worry with Mr. Foljambe," said Mrs. Graydon. "I detest that man."

"Shouldn't I like to put a little prussic-acid on his tongue?" said George.

"George, please don't say such things," said Eleanor, "I thought you knew nothing about him."

"Oh, did you!" said George. "Trust mamma for keeping anything from me that I have a mind to find out!"

Mrs. Graydon looked confused, and said, "He promised not to tell."

"But," persisted Eleanor, "you told Miss Clairvaux you knew nothing about it."

"We doctors, my dear child, think nothing of such a white lie as that, and have to tell plenty of them. I had already promised mamma not to say I knew, so how was I to get out of it?"

"Ah, one false step always leads to another. People are sure to be found out."

"Where was the false step? A letter came from Meadowleigh, and, of course, I expected to know what was in it. Mamma said 'it is about Miss Clairvaux's private concerns; so, of course, you will be upon honour.' 'Of course,' said I. So that was all."

"Write again to Miss Clairvaux, Eleanor," said Mrs. Graydon. "Tell her we are anxious."

"Yes, mamma, I will." The letter was written and sent. Still no answer: and as more than a fortnight had now elapsed, and Eleanor's health and spirits were restored, it was agreed between her and her mother that she had better return to her kind protectress without waiting for a summons.

There was no pang, this time, in the parting between mother and daughter. They were cheerful and hopeful, for was not Eleanor on the path of Duty? and she found it a pleasant one.

> Stern lawgiver! yet thou dost wear
> The Godhead's most benignant grace;
> Nor know we anything so fair
> As is the smile upon thy face.

The journey appeared much shorter to Eleanor, now that she knew the line, than when it was new and strange; and she noted with surprise and delight the progress vegetation had made during her short absence. The oaks, ashes, and beeches were now in full leaf, the hedges vivid green, the hay nearly ready to cut, the birds in full song; and, at the first pause, she heard the cuckoo.

When Meadowleigh appeared in sight, she noted with the partiality of an acquaintance amid what had formerly been to her a confused cluster of white and red-brick tenements, the grey steeple of the parish-church, the red-brick meeting-house, the tall chimnies of Miss Thompson's school, the massive front of Mr. Debenham's family mansion, the ivy-covered vicarage with its southern wall famous for apricots; the cricket-field, and the field where men played quoits on Saturday afternoons, and schoolboys flew their kites; intersected by the gravelled church-path. Happily for the artist, Meadowleigh was as yet unspoilt by building societies and their freehold tenements; but there was a large piece of ground apportioned into gardens on the allotment system, which, in spite of its productive crops, was rather an eye-sore to Eleanor. She thought it a nicer plan for poor people to have good gardens round their own cottages, for their apple-trees, bee-hives, and even pig-sties, if not too near the house. All these little matters she now noted and brooded upon at her ease, with a mind at leisure from itself.

She left her light box at the station, to be forwarded when convenient, and proceeded on foot to the Peaked House. The railway-wires were giving forth that strange, wild, pathetic music which seems like the voice of Nature herself, breathing through her works; and she thought of Prospero's haunted island

Full of sweet airs, that give delight and hurt not.

It was a pleasant walk, and, as it happened, perfectly lonely; she did not meet a creature.

Arrived at the house, she looked at the various windows for the chance of a glimpse of Miss Clairvaux. No one was visible; there were no blinds drawn down, to betoken illness or absence, but all the windows were shut, which was not in accordance with Miss Clairvaux's airy habits. The gravel walk was untidy with weeds; and some coloured print aprons were spread on the grass to dry.

Eleanor knocked and rang, on which Fly began to bark as if he would split his throat; and, after a lengthened delay, an old woman opened the door.

" Is Miss Clairvaux at home ?" said Eleanor, with a strange misgiving of something wrong.

" No, miss."

" Where is she gone ?"

" Can't say, miss."

" When will she come back ?"

" Don't know, miss."

" Where's Claudia ?"

" Gone home, miss."

" Where's Hester ?"

" Gone home too, miss."

"Dear me, this seems very strange. Let me come in, please—I want to sit down and consider what to do."

The old woman seemed to think this might as well be done standing as sitting, and stood in the doorway, completely filling it up.

" I live here," said Eleanor impatiently.

"You may as well let me in. Is the house let?"

"No, miss."

"Then why do you keep me out of it?"

"I was told to let nobody in, miss."

"Who by?"

"The gentleman."

"What gentleman?"

"Mr. Foljambe's his name, miss."

Eleanor's heart gave a great throb.

"Where's Claudia?" said she, in a thick voice. "Where does she live?"

"Down the green lane, miss. There's only one house."

"I'll go to her."

The old woman seemed relieved by this decision; and closed the door in her face. Eleanor, with tightened breath and unquiet mien, hastened to the 'green lane,' which was one of her favourite walks. A thatched cottage, buried in apple-trees, stood at the lower-end. She raised the latch of the neat little white gate, and tapped at the door, which was opened by Claudia, who held some coarse needlework in her hand.

"O, Miss Graydon! I'm so glad to see you!" exclaimed Claudia, who immediately began to cry.

"What's all this about? Where's Miss Clairvaux?"

"That's the very thing I don't know, miss. Come in, please, miss, and sit down; you don't look very well."

Eleanor gladly did so. "Tell me all you know," said she.

"I know very little, miss," said Claudia, "leastways, very little I can make head or tail of. Two or three days after you went to London, two gentlemen called and desired to see Miss Clairvaux, they gave me no names. Mistress desired me to ask their names, so then they sent in cards. I don't know what was on them. I thought she looked as if she did not know them, and I waited in the hall, suppos-

ing they had come to collect for some subscription. In about ten minutes, or a quarter
of an hour, I can't justly say which, she rang
the bell pretty smartly, and they came out
rather brisk, and I let them out. I didn't
notice anything particular. But when I went
into the parlour, I saw mistress looked
troubled, and she said, ' I can't think what
those men came for, nor who sent them.'
She called them *men*, but I had took them
for gentlemen. I said, ' didn't they come
to collect for a subscription, ma'am ?' She
said, ' oh no, nothing of the sort—they only
came to ask impertinent questions, I think—'
and stood in a painful sort of a muse. It
seemed to me strange, and I hoped they might
not be any of the swell mob, they looked
better than that ; but yet I looked closer than
usual that night, to all the fastenings. And
then I thought no more about it. I don't
know whether mistress did. Well, a few
days passed on, and it was on a Wednesday

or a Thursday, I forget which, that a railway
boy came up to the house with a small brown
paper parcel, that seemed only to hold a
letter; and when he had been paid and sent
away, and Miss Clairvaux had read the letter,
she told me to put on my bonnet directly
and run down to Mr. Debenham and ask him
to come up to her immediately; and as I was
setting off, she cried after me, ' tell him it is
very pressing,' so I never stayed even to pin
my shawl but ran off.   And just at the turn
of the paling, I came upon an old woman—
that old woman that's now in the house,
carrying a small bundle of things tied up in
a red pocket-handkerchief, and a little farther
on, I came upon a close fly, and, looking into
it as I passed, saw Mr. Foljambe inside it,
and another person that didn't look like a
gentleman.   Directly I saw Mr. Foljambe, I
felt sure something was going wrong; for you
see, miss, without ever having heard anything
direct from Miss Clairvaux about him, I

know they can't bear one another, and that she's somehow in his power, and he wishes her ill. So I saw the need for my bringing Mr. Debenham to her as fast as I could; and really I flew rather than ran, and could hardly speak when I got to the house.

"To my great disappointment, miss, the housemaid told me Mr. Debenham and his mother were spending a few days at the sea-side. So then I did not know whether to run back or go to somebody else; but I thought there could be no harm in fetching the doctor, so I went to Mr. Burrowes; but he hadn't come in from his morning round. So then I went back. When I got home, I had to wait ever so long before I was let in; there was no sign of the fly anywhere, only I could see the marks where the wheels had turned round, right in front of the gate. At last, as I kept ringing, the door was opened a little bit, and who should open it but that old woman! I stared, just for a

moment, and darted in, to go to Miss Clairvaux; but the old woman called after me,
'It's no good your going to look after her,
for she's gone.' 'Gone?' says I, 'where?'
'With her friends, I suppose,' says she.
'She's got no friends,' said I. 'That's a
bad job,' said the old woman. 'That is, she
has heaps of friends,' said I, 'for she's the
friend of everybody; but she never goes
visiting them, and I'm sure she hadn't such
a thought in her head when I left her just
now.' 'Maybe so,' said the old woman,
'and yet summat may have happened since.'
'Where's Hester?' said I. 'Gone to her
home,' said the old woman, 'and you're to
go to yours.' 'And who's to pay me my
wages?' said I. 'Miss Clairvaux herself,
when she comes back, I suppose,' said she.
'When will she come back?' said I. 'I
know no more than you,' said she; 'I never
spoke to her in my life—you needn't go
up-stairs; for I'm left in charge.' 'But I

must fetch my things,' said I; and I ran into one room after another, and saw everything in confusion; and then I ran up-stairs and found the rooms locked up and sealed. 'Well,' thinks I, 'here's been quick work!'"

"Quick, indeed!" ejaculated Eleanor, who had been careful not to interrupt her. "Well; and then—"

"Well; and then," pursued Claudia, "I stood still for a minute, by my bed-side, all in a maze, and began to cry; but that would do no good, only I couldn't make it all out— it wasn't a bit like Miss Clairvaux to go off in that way, leaving everything at sixes and sevens; and yet, how could I tell but something in the letter had put her out of the way, and summoned her off at a moment's notice to the death-bed of some relation or such-like?"

"She has no relation," said Eleanor.

"Well, miss, I didn't know of any; but what could I think, and what was I to do?

There were all the rooms locked up but the attic; and Hester's things gone, and the old woman's bundle set on the bed, and the old woman herself standing in the doorway, saying, 'What are you waiting for?' 'I'm waiting to turn things in my mind,' says I, quite sharp. 'O well, then when you've turned them, you'll let me know,' says she, sitting down on the bed, 'and the sooner the better, for this is my room now.' 'Did Miss Clairvaux say so?' says I. 'Who else should?' says she. So, there was I shut up; but yet I suspected she was a false old woman, and only deceiving me. So I packed up my things as fast as I could. and then thought, 'Where on earth am I to go?' For I've no more friends, miss, than Miss Clairvaux, nor yet any enemies. I felt forlorn, that's what I did! but I didn't choose to shew it. So I carried my things down, and looked in again at the parlour, where one would think there'd been a scuffle, for a chair was upset, a sofa-cushion on the ground, and the hearth-rug in a rumple. 'Don't go in there,' cries the old woman, stumping down after me, 'I'm arranging the things.' 'One would think you'd been *dis*-arranging them!' said I; and I gave her such a look !—

"Then," resumed Claudia, with a deep sigh, "I took up my little box and lifted it outside; but I said, 'My big box is too heavy for me to carry—I must get a man to fetch it.' 'You may as well set it outside,' says the old woman, 'for nobody will touch it. I'll lend you a hand to get it down stairs.' I thought she might as well as not; so we carried it down between us, and set it outside; and then I came to Thomas Ford, to ask him to fetch it. He and his wife were just sitting down to a beefsteak pudding; and when I asked him to carry my box, they said, 'what, are you leaving your place?' so then I began to cry. When I told them all about it, they *did* stare! Mrs. Ford says, ' well, whatever you do, you'll want a dinner first; so sit down and have a bit with us.' But I felt as if I couldn't swallow, and would sooner have gone back to my box. But Master Ford says, ' If you're not hungry, you know, I am, and must eat my dinner now it's dished; so do take a bit for company.' So I took a bit for company, and then Mrs. Ford said in her kind way, ' well, it seems a strange affair, Claudia, and you're clearly much to be pitied, and perhaps Miss Clairvaux may need to be pitied, too; but you're welcome to sleep and board here for the present, till you've time to look about you; and we can settle for it when convenient.' So that's what I've done."

CHAPTER III.

Anticipation is the presage of a truth before it is fairly proved.—WHEWELL.

A PAINFUL pause ensued.

"Well," said Eleanor, "it seems the strangest, the saddest thing I ever knew. Do they say anything about it in the town ?"

"O yes, miss, they say all manner of things. But they know nothing."

" What sort of things do they say ?"

"Some of them," said Claudia, blushing vividly, " say it's like as if she were took off

D 2

to an asylum. But you know, miss, she is not mad!"

"Certainly not. Who dares to say such a wicked thing?"

"Nobody that I know of, but them that consorts with Mr. Horsefield."

"Mr. Horsefield! Is *he* down here?"

"He has been, at any rate, miss, as busy as a bluebottle in a larder. His maggots are hatched now."

"He's a bad young man, I'm afraid."

"You may say that, miss! I hate him like a spider, that's what I do."

"Don't the gentry take it up?"

"I don't know whether it's reached up to them yet, miss. You see they don't hear things as soon as we do. Many of them make a merit of it."

Eleanor knew this was true.

"Those of the gossipping sort, such as Mrs. Plover," added Claudia, "mostly take things up just in the way they shouldn't be taken."

This was true too.

"I can't think what to do!" exclaimed Eleanor. "Something ought to be done."

"That's just what I think, miss, only, who by? Miss Clairvaux, you see, was never for being very thick with her neighbours; so that they think it no business of theirs. I dare say they say to one another, 'it's very sad; but her own relations must know how to manage her best.' Don't you think so, miss?"

"I am afraid it may be so, indeed!"

"Especially in anything that might get them into a scrape. Gentlefolks is mostly afraid of burning their fingers, miss!"

"Not Miss Clairvaux."

"No," said Claudia with emotion. "She would always burn her fingers for anybody; and now, perhaps, it is laid to her charge."

"Where's Hester?" cried Eleanor suddenly. "She must know what passed in your absence."

"Hester's at the greengrocer's, miss. No, she knows nothing. She had gone into the garden to gather peas. When she came in, there was no one in the house but the old woman and Mr. Foljambe. He said to her, 'Miss Clairvaux has been suddenly called away. This person is left in sole charge till she returns, and you and your fellow servant are to go away at once.' And then he hurried out of the house. Hester is a timid girl, and slow of speech, and could not get out 'may I not stay till Claudia comes back?' till he had banged the door after him, and the old woman would not let her."

"How unfortunate that Mr. Debenham should be away!"

"He's at home now, miss! He was to come home last night."

"Indeed! Oh, then I will go to him at once."

"I'm so glad!" said Claudia. "You think, then, he can do something?"

"Indeed, Claudia, I do not know; but it is worth trying. It is the only thing I can think of. Give me a little water, please."

"You look sadly excited, miss—won't you have a slice of bread and butter?"

"No, thank you. I feel as if I could not eat."

"Ah! I know that feeling," said Claudia.

Eleanor hastily drank the glass of sparkling water, ice-cold from the deep well, and then started on her mission. It was now nearly one o'clock, and the sun was very hot, but she walked very fast, regardless of the heat, up the steep lane and along the shadeless road. Swiftly-rolling wheels presently gained on her from behind—the doctor's chaise, with Mr. Burrowes in it. He bowed to her as he passed.

"Mr. Burrowes! Mr. Burrowes!" cried Eleanor, running after him. He heard her, and checked his horse.

"I beg your pardon, but I want particularly

to speak to you. Do pray oblige me for a few minutes."

"You look ready to drop," said he pity-ingly, "and I have not much time to spare. Step into the chaise, and we can talk as we go along. My groom shall follow me—he knows where I am bound."

The man got out, and Eleanor got in, with-out the least hesitation. They drove off at a moderate pace.

" Oh," said she gratefully, " I am so obliged to you ! I am quite at my wit's end about Miss Clairvaux."

" Ah, so is everybody," said Mr. Burrowes, with great interest in his manner. " I shall be very glad to hear the rights of it from you."

" I know nothing—that's the worst of it ! I was away at the time, most unfortunately. I had not been quite well; and Miss Clairvaux most kindly sent me home. While with my mother, I frequently wrote ; but received no answers. This appeared to us so strange, so unlike Miss Clairvaux, that we became uneasy, and thought something had happened—"

" What did you think had happened ?"

" I cannot specify any particular fear ; but I had a general feeling of uneasiness, because, shortly before I left her, Miss Clairvaux had had some words with Mr. Foljambe."

" What were those words about ?"

" I am not sure," said Eleanor, hesitatingly, " that I am at liberty to tell."

"There is a well-known axiom," returned Mr. Burrowes, who was now driving very slowly, " that one should have no secrets from one's lawyer, one's confessor, or one's medical man."

" Only it is not my secret !—However," pursued she, " I am not sure that it is any secret at all, or, at least, that Miss Clairvaux would make it one, or wish me to do so in the present instance—"

"Settle it your own way, my dear Miss Graydon."

Eleanor revolved it a little in her mind.
"I am sure," she said, presently, "that
she has a high opinion of your honour
and judgment—I think she would trust
you—I'm sure *I* should—yes, I will."

He smiled a little, and did not seem surprised at the result.

"The words were about money matters—"

"Words often are."

"Ever since I had been with Miss Clairvaux, there had been something at issue between them, which seemed to trouble her.
She did not tell me what it was; but the
very first evening of my being at the Peaked
House, she asked me, while she was direct-
ing a letter, whether I did not think Foljambe an ugly name; and afterwards,
whether I were in the habit of re-writing
letters."

"Re-writing letters?"

"She said she often wrote and re-wrote
letters, toning them down each time."

"I wish the habit were more common," said Mr. Burrowes smiling. "Go on—you interest me very much. Allow me one word— you spoke just now of 'ever since you had been with Miss Clairvaux.' Were you with her as being her relative, her friend—or, or only —"

"Her companion," answered Eleanor, smiling a little at the adroitness with which he made his professional character an excuse for solving a doubt that puzzled all the gossips in the neighbourhood.

"Just so—I was in hopes—if you had been a relative, you see, your position would have given you some colour for interference in the present matter, which otherwise —— Were you placed about her by Mr. Foljambe?"

"Mr. Foljambe? Dear me, no!" exclaimed Eleanor. "What call had Mr. Foljambe to place anybody about her? Her position was quite independent. I had never even heard his name till I went to her."

"Ah, ah, just so. Dear me, dear me—you are quite in Miss Clairvaux's interest then, of course; as I supposed —"

"Quite entirely so! I have every reason to be; for her goodness to me has been unexampled."

"She wanted to have you about her, I suppose, for an ally, a witness, a protectress, in case of any —"

"O no, no, nothing of the sort! She wanted nothing of the kind! She was expecting no such catastrophe as this. She had me down solely for my good—solely because she heard I was in want of a situation."

"She could not have made a happier choice, I am sure," said Mr. Burrowes feelingly.

"There was no choice in the matter," said Eleanor with quickness. "It was pure benevolence. She happened to hear through a correspondent that an amiable artist had died, leaving his wife and daughter unprovided, and that the daughter was looking out for a situation. I was that daughter. Miss Clairvaux interested herself about it, and thought she had secured me a situation. It proved that she was mistaken. So then, rather than that I should be disappointed, she resolved to have me to live with her, and to give me the salary I should have had of the lady who put me off. I had not the remotest idea how it was, when I came down. Otherwise, of course, I could not have accepted her kindness. When I asked her, the second day, 'what my duties were,' she said, 'my dear, you have only to please yourself; this is Liberty Hall. You advertised, did you not, that you wished to live with an elderly lady? Well, you *are* living with an elderly lady.'"

"Extraordinary! most extraordinary," repeated Mr. Burrowes.

"And," continued Eleanor, with tears in her eyes, "no one can tell, as I can, of the beauty of her daily life—her thoughtlessness of self—her thoughtfulness for others."

"I can readily believe all that," said Mr. Burrowes, "but have you never observed any little aberrations, any—"

"Never! never!"

"Well, I'm very glad indeed to hear it, for I never observed anything of the sort myself, but there are extraordinary stories about, and how they should have arisen—"

"I believe Mr. Horsefield set them about."

"Mr. Horsefield? who's he?"

"A low attorney's clerk, employed by Mr. Foljambe. He came in one day, when Miss Clairvaux was out, and I was at home, and, not knowing I was in the house, began tampering with the maid-servant."

"Ha! Miss Graydon, your testimony begins to be important. What did he say?"

"He said—my head is so confused that I cannot just now recall distinctly what he said," returned poor Eleanor, "though I believe if I were more collected I should remember his very words, they surprised me so. I remember he began by saying, 'how has the old lady been going on lately?' It startled me, for I did not know there was a man in the house, and I could not think how he had got in, nor who he could mean. I heard the housemaid (Claudia, you know her, I dare say?")

"Oh yes."

"I heard her say in a frightened kind of way, 'I don't know what you mean, sir.' And then he offered her a bribe, saying 'Here's something to sharpen your wits.'"

"Impudent dog!" exclaimed Mr. Burrowes, out of patience. "Why, here seems

to have been a regular conspiracy. Miss
Graydon, have you any more to tell?"

"Oh yes, this is only the beginning!—"

"Your pardon, then, one instant. I am
going to make a call on the very man to help
you:—a humourist, a hypochondriac, but a
man who knows everything; of immense
powers, if he would but use them, and with
nothing to prevent his using them but his own
will. His benevolence is immense, he can see
farther into a millstone than anybody I know,
and, in short, if you can get him to undertake the matter, he will very likely carry it
through."

Eleanor had been talking so eagerly, that
she had not taken the least note of anything
around her; and now she perceived that Mr.
Burrowes was driving up to the entrance of
the secluded old house, with the high garden
walls capped with funereal urns, inhabited
by the mysterious recluse; and that Mr.
Burrowes' groom, who had taken some short

cut, was awaiting his master at the gate.

"Who do you mean?" said she in a flutter.

"Mr. Newland," he replied. "He's a capital old gentleman, though a curious one. In his youth he read law, and entered at Lincoln's Inn, but never practised. He preaches, however, if he does not practise, and writes stinging newspaper articles, under the signature of Vindex. Oh, his invectives are felt far and wide, I assure you! Now, all you have to do—"

"Oh, I'd rather not go in," cried Eleanor, hastily.

"All you have to do," pursued Mr. Burrowes, without noticing her shrinking, "if you mean to help your friend, is to tell him the whole story just as you were telling it to me. What! won't you do this much for your benefactress? You need not be afraid of him—only his husk is rough: there's a sound, sweet nut inside. If you won't make the venture, 'pon my soul I don't see what's to be done. It's more in his way than mine."

"Oh, I don't mind venturing, only—he'll think it so strange—"

"He'll think the story you have to tell him strange, I'll answer for it," said Mr. Burrowes, giving the reins to his man, and stepping out. "Come!" he added, holding out his hand to her. She gave him hers.

CHAPTER IV.

Duke.—But what said Jacques?

ELEANOR scarcely took notice of the garish gleam of the old-fashioned garden within the gloomy walls, as she followed Mr. Burrowes up the wide, shallow steps to the beetling door-way, where an old man-servant in a nondescript livery looked astounded at her appearance, and bestowed on Mr. Burrowes a glance of mute remonstrance. Without heeding him, Mr. Burrowes hastily crossed the square hall, paved in diamonds with white and

E 2

black marble, and passed the open door of a dining-parlour, where covers were laid for two.

He opened a second door, and, looking in, was greeted with a pleasantly spoken—

"Just in time, Mr. Doctor, to save our roast from spoiling," when, catching a glimpse of Eleanor's light muslin, the speaker abruptly changed his note, exclaiming :—

"What, what, what, what ? . . . . . a woman, sir? a woman? stop, stop, I say; stop !—"

And Eleanor, to her amusement, beheld the flying skirts of an old gentleman's flowered dressing-gown in full retreat; the door closing on him before she had a glimpse of his countenance. Her next feeling was of great embarrassment.

" I really must go," she energetically whispered to Mr. Burrowes, " I ought not to have come in."

" Hush, hush, never mind," returned he, putting up his finger. " All will come

right, you'll see. Just sit down a moment." And handing her a newspaper, he
hastily followed his patient. Eleanor was
in no cue for newspaper reading; she felt
most uncomfortable; and as the *séance* was
prolonged, had more than half a mind to steal
away; but how pass that grim porter at the
door?

She heard their voices in the next room;
but the walls and doors were of such old-
fashioned thickness that they did not betray a
syllable of what was said. Mr. Burrowes,
however, seemed to be holding forth : perhaps
on the recluse's want of due appreciation of
the softer sex. Suspense made the delay seem
longer to Eleanor than it really was; and she
asked herself whether Mr. Burrowes could
have forgotten her altogether, and be relating
in detail all the news of the parish.

In truth, this was what the worthy doctor
was usually in the habit of doing; thereby
putting the old gentleman who was supposed

to know nothing quite *au courant du jour ;* and this was one main reason why Mr. Newland valued his visits, and affected to consider himself in want of them ; whereas he knew pretty well that his valetudinarianism was mainly an excuse for the indulgence of his peculiar habits. While revolving in his mind schemes for the benefit of mankind, he felt infinite contempt for that portion of it within his immediate reach, and would by no means sacrifice his darling peace and quiet to the senseless, slavish forms of society he so detested.

A dead pause ensued ; and Eleanor began to think they must both have retired to some remoter room. Suddenly, the door opened ; and the old gentleman stood before her, not in his flowered dressing-gown, but spruce as a beau, in a faultless suit of black. His hair was white as snow, and so were his bushy eyebrows ; but in the hollow caverns beneath them gleamed dark eyes, that just now were full of fire.

"Young lady," said he, with a formal bow, and then advancing and holding out his hand to her, not without grace, " my good young lady, you honour me by this proof of confidence. Our good friend, Burrowes, has repeated to me all you were so obliging as to communicate to him; but the story remains unfinished. I wish to trouble you for the rest. Take your time, my dear, take your time! there is not the least hurry—"

The peculiar major-domo here put in his head, and oracularly said,

" The lamb-chops is dished."

"Dish the lamb-chops!" said Mr. Newland with asperity; on which the major-domo, again looking astounded, withdrew.

"Perhaps we can lunch and talk at the same time?" suggested Mr. Burrowes.

" No, no, no, no, no," answered the old gentleman rapidly, "one thing at a time will last the longer. Now, my dear, I am all attention."

He seated himself opposite to her as he spoke, with his arms crossed before him on his library table, his chin resting on his hands, and his eyes fixed full on her. She faltered, looked down, and said,

"I forget where I am to go on."

"About Mr. Horsefield," suggested Mr. Burrowes.

"Oh yes—about Mr. Horsefield. Mr. Horsefield came again, some time afterwards, and found Miss Clairvaux at home, but not alone. My mother, brother, and myself were with her. She seemed surprised at his intrusion, and told him she could not be delayed, as we were all going together to the railway station. He said he would not detain her a moment, as he only wanted her signature to a paper; half drawing it from his pocket as he spoke. She replied, with decision, that she should not think of signing a paper without reading it first."

"Right, right. And then—"

"And then he went away."

"This Mr. Foljambe is Miss Clairvaux's brother, is not he?"

"No, sir; no relation."

"No relation?"

Eleanor explained the connexion, adding, "Though Miss Clairvaux had the independent use of what came to her through her mother, she told me that what was derived from her step-father came to her through his son, and depended on certain conditions, very unlikely to deprive her of it."

"And you don't know those conditions?"

"Yes sir, I do now. On her sanity."

"Aye, aye?" exclaimed Mr. Newland, looking excited, while Mr. Burrowes also appeared keenly interested. "We are bringing it to a point now. How came the question of sanity to be at all raised?"

"He —— Will you please, sir, to let me go strait on?"

"Yes, yes, tell it your own way."

"One evening, after a very eventful scene, Miss Clairvaux told me all the particulars of the singular position in which she was placed. Her father, a very good young clergyman, returning home late one night from visiting a dying person, by mistake walked over the river's brink and was drowned. The verdict at the inquest was simply 'found drowned,' it could be nothing more; but, strangely enough, Mrs. Clairvaux's second husband took it into his head that Mr. Clairvaux must have committed suicide, and on this he based a theory of insanity, which led to the provision in his will, that his step-daughter was to have the uncontrolled possession of what he left her, except in the case of her becoming deranged, in which case it was to be administered by his son Jasper."

"Stop!" cried Mr. Newland abruptly. "You have told me all this very clearly, but I am afraid of a treacherous memory; I must make a note or two."

And he rapidly wrote down the substance of all she had been saying, and continued to note the heads of what she said afterwards. What would have frightened Eleanor very much at the beginning of the interview, now inspired her with confidence.

" You spoke just now," said he, reviewing his memoranda, " of Miss Clairvaux having related this to you one evening after a very eventful scene. What was it ?"

" Sir, I had returned from a walk, and was surprised at a man's voice in the house. The housemaid told me it was Mr. Foljambe ; so I went up to my room, concluding him to be speaking to Miss Clairvaux on business. I could hear their voices in the room beneath. They seemed raised a little, and gradually grew louder, as if in dispute. Suddenly there was a sharp cry, as if of pain, and Miss Clairvaux came into the hall and called aloud, ' Eleanor ! Eleanor ! are you at home ? Come down to me directly !' "

From this point Eleanor's account became so vivid as to be little short of dramatic. Her eyes kindled, her cheeks burned as she spoke. When she got to Mr. Foljambe's exasperating, "see for yourself under what excitement she is ! look at her swelling veins ! her flushed complexion !" Mr. Newland could bear it no longer, he started to his feet, exclaiming :

" Atrocious rascal !"

—sat down again, applied his handkerchief to his face, made rapid additions to his notes, and then, looking up at her, said, "go on."

At this instant, the peculiar major-domo again inserted his physiognomy, which this time had something truly piteous in its expression, and said :

" Sir, the asparagus will be quite spoilt."

"And really, sir," said Mr. Burrowes, " Miss Graydon begins to look exhausted, and has had a great deal to try her this morning; so that I advise we should all adjourn to lunch."

"Well, well, well," said Mr. Newland, reluctantly, "we will come, then; we will come. Covers for three, John, covers for three."

On which, John, relieved, but again astounded, briskly withdrew to make the requisite additions to the table.

"We shall easily resume the thread," murmured Mr. Newland to himself, in a manner that had become habitual to him, as he looked over his notes, "we shall easily resume the thread—and people must live, people must live. Accept my arm, my dear; an old man's arm, that has not had a young girl's hand upon it for many a year." He gently pressed it as he spoke. Eleanor felt quite touched. He inspired her with inexpressible trust: they seemed quite to understand one another's natures already.

Mr. Burrowes, with secret satisfaction,

followed them into the dining-room; for he was accustomed to partake of Mr. Newland's neat little lunches pretty frequently; and he was not so absorbed in Miss Clairvaux's affairs, though he was unaffectedly interested in them, as to feel indifferent to the condition in which the lamb and asparagus might appear on table. Three fried whiting, 'one for manners,' for whom a consumer was now provided unexpectedly, seemed none the worse for delay; and the old gentleman gaily pressed and smiled, seeming a valetudinarian in nothing but his toast-and-water.

"One glass of sherry to-day, sir," said Mr. Burrowes.

"Well, Burrowes, it must be *but* one, then, to pledge this fair young lady."

The luncheon was really a much needed restorative to Eleanor, whom the heat and hurry of her walk, combined with previous agitation, had nearly overpowered. She said little while it lasted, leaving the two gentle-

men to support a trivial chat while the foot-
man remained in the room. But in truth,
they found so much to consider in what they
were eating, or in what they had been hearing, that they chiefly spoke in monosyllables.
John, meanwhile, stood in absorbed con-
templation of Eleanor, being intent on giving
an exact description of her to ' his old woman '
—the dresser of the whiting—who was the
only female on the premises, and always
lived out of sight.

After the gooseberry tart was removed,
John put wine and biscuits before his master,
and disappeared.

" Shall we resume our talk here?" said Mr.
Newland, " or return to the study ? I think
we are very comfortable here. You will
oblige me, Burrowes, by bringing me my
memoranda —"

" Let me go, sir," said Eleanor ; and
before he could say no, she was gone.

" Why, what a tripping fairy you are !"

said he when she came back. "I should have liked you for my partner in the days when I was as light-footed as you are, and could dance all night."

She smiled.

"I suppose that was before I was born, sir."

"Fie, fie! why should you put me in mind how old I am?

> "And said I that my limbs were old?
> And said I that my heart was cold?

"All owing to the glass of sherry, Burrowes, that you *would* make me take. (A truce with foolery.) Now, to resume the story of this poor lady —"

"It is almost ended, sir. We were a good deal disturbed by this scene with Mr. Foljambe; but after his departure, we persuaded ourselves that no more would come of it, in spite of what he had said about 'placing the matter in proper hands.' That expression had vaguely alarmed me at first; but Miss Clairvaux looked on it only as an idle threat. We soon forgot it—that is, after she had made me write a full account of what had passed to my mother, who had inspired her with great affection and confidence."

"As is the mother, so is the daughter," muttered Mr. Newland. "Well?"

"Miss Clairvaux gave me leave to spend a short time at home, of which I gladly availed myself. I wrote to her frequently, according to her desire; but to my surprise received no answers. Becoming uneasy, I resolved to return to her, fearing she might be ill. I came down this morning."

She then related how surprised she had been to find the Peaked House in the sole keeping of the old woman; and how painfully her surprise and alarm had been increased by what she had heard from Claudia. The muscles of Mr. Newland's face worked as she

proceeded. When she mentioned the signs of
a scuffle in the parlour, he ejaculated—

"Poor soul! poor soul! who knows what she
may have suffered! what indignities they may
have put upon her!"

Then smiting the table with his fist, he exclaimed,—"This is just such a case as I should
like to expose!'

"Precisely such a case as the pen of Vindex
can make effective," said Mr. Burrowes.

"Softly, softly," said Mr. Newland to him,
calming himself. "There is a great deal to
be thought of before the pen is used at all.
There are two important facts to be ascertained before we can tell that there even *is* a
case. Firstly, that Miss Clairvaux is at this
moment in confinement: secondly, that she
does not deserve or need to be so."

He looked from one to the other.

"I am sure she does not, sir!" said
Eleanor with confidence. "I, who have lived
with her should know!"

" I like your tone, my dear."

" It would be well worth while, sir, I should think," said Mr. Burrowes, " if one could rummage up some facts about the Clairvauxes: whether there really were hereditary insanity among them—whether Mr. Clairvaux's death could anyhow be cleared up."

" I have thought of that already, Burrowes. It will be quite worth while, if necessary. But, firstly; how do we know that Miss Clairvaux is not at this moment taking her ease at her inn? or sitting beside the death-bed of some old friend or near relation ?"

" She has none, sir," said Eleanor. " Once, when she was saying she wondered how people could submit their photographs to the mercy of their common acquaintance, and that they ought to be restricted to dear friends, she said, with a little sigh, ' there is not one living person to whom I should care to give such a pledge—unless you, Eleanor. ' "

"But where *is* she?" ssid Mr. Burrowes.
"She must be somewhere."

"Aye, Burrowes, that's a trueism," said
Mr. Newland, "and I think we are quite jus-
tified, as humane neighbours of hers, in inquiring where? We must be careful not to be
found hunting for a mare's nest. As Miss
Clairvaux, a lady very generally respected, has
suddenly disappeared from among us, and is
known by her household to have had no
thought, or made any preparation for going, it
is natural for us, merely as humane neighbours,
to take steps to learn whither she is gone:
which steps must be taken prudently and
quietly. Mr. Foljambe was the last person
seen with her: Mr. Foljambe must know where
she is. I am fully determined to see this
matter to an end, and shall have no objection
to appear openly in it at the proper time: but
at present, it is not necessary for me to do so.
This young lady depones to having written
several letters to Miss Clairvaux, which were

not answered: probably they never reached her. It is very natural, for this young lady—(Eleanor, I think you call yourself, my dear? Eleanor Graydon? a very pretty name), it is very natural for you to be surprised at getting no answer, and at wishing to know, since Miss Clairvaux is not to be found, what has become of your letters. Would you object to write this, merely as a matter of inquiry, to Mr. Foljambe?"

"Not if you think I had better do so, sir."

"I do think so. Let us adjourn to the study, which is cooler and shadier than this room, and we shall there find pen, ink, and paper."

CHAPTER V.

How various his employments, whom the world
Calls idle! and who justly, in return,
Esteems that busy world an idler too.

THE study was indeed cool and shady,
looking out into a garden with gay flower-
beds and turfen alleys with pleached hedges,
fit for Beatrice and Benedick, though seques-
trated to the pastime of an invalid old man.
Seclusion could not have looked more cheerful.
The lofty ceiling of the study was fretted with
ornaments which, though only of plaster, had
a quaint and rich effect. The carved mantel-

piece was six feet high. The walls were covered with books, pictures, and prints, and the tables were loaded with papers; but the furniture was destitute of gloss, and the carpet worn threadbare.

Eleanor sat down to a sheet of the best note-paper, much larger than she was accustomed to use; and took up a quill pen.

" What date shall I put ?" said she.

" Stonewall House, if you will," said Mr. Newland, with a sarcastic smile. " That will surprise him a little."

" Why not date from the Peaked House ? or from Mr. Debenham's ?" said Mr. Burrowes.

" Why should I ?" said Eleanor, in surprise. " It would not be true."

" Right, young lady," said Mr. Newland, approvingly.

" Would not Meadowleigh be sufficient ?"

" Let the date stand over for the present."

Eleanor complied, and wrote the note

without pausing; then handed it for approval to Mr. Newland, who read it through his double eye-glass.

"A good hand—a good hand," muttered he, "and hand-writing shows character. Here is a man's firmness and a woman's delicacy."

The note ran as follows:

"July 15th, 18—

"Sir,

"On returning to Meadowleigh, I find Miss Clairvaux has left it, and that the Peaked House is at present in your charge. May I trouble you to inform me where to address Miss Clairvaux, and also what has become of several letters of mine which have been posted to the Peaked House since Miss Clairvaux went away? There is property of mine now locked up there, with your seal on the door.

"Your obedient servant,

"ELEANOR GRAYDON."

"That last sentence is capital," said Mr. Newland, chuckling, as he handed the letter to Mr. Burrowes. "She has a fair claim on him for her property."

"Certainly," said Mr. Burrowes; "but I won't answer for his telling her where Miss Clairvaux is."

"Supposing," said Eleanor, "that Mr. Foljambe had, or made a pretext for putting Miss Clairvaux under restraint, what are the forms he would have to go through?"

"Aye, Burrowes, tell us that," said Mr. Newland, looking at him keenly.

"Well, I don't know that I am quite prepared to say," said Mr. Burrowes, attentively considering the formation of his nails.

"Just such an answer as I expected you to make," said Mr. Newland, triumphantly. "The amount of general ignorance on this subject is as unaccountable as it is disgraceful."

"My dear sir, *you* are the only man who

know everything! Happily my practice has not at all lain in this line. And besides, when I observed that I was not prepared to say, of course, all I meant was that I needed a little consideration first. Oh, certainly, I can give you some information on the subject. If a patient is to be subjected to treatment of this peculiar kind, an order, you know, must be made out."

"Just so. What sort of order?"

"Well, an order stating certain particulars, and so forth, and signed by some relation or friend—"

"Mr. Foljambe, strictly speaking, is neither," said Eleanor, in an under tone.

"And besides that, there must be two certificates, signed by two medical men unconnected with each other, and who have had no previous consultation or meeting. Oh, the liberty of the British subject has been carefully provided for!"

"In theory, not always in practice. Now,

I happen to know," said Mr. Newland, leaning complacently back in his chair, resting
his elbows on its two arms, and joining his
forefingers together, "that a well filled-up
certificate of this kind is the exception rather
than the rule."

"Didn't I tell you," said Mr. Burrowes
in a half-aside to Eleanor, "that here was
a man that knew everything?"

"Pish," said Mr. Newland peevishly.
"Did you ever sign a certificate of this kind,
Mr. Doctor, yourself?"

"No, sir, I never was called on, luckily.
Bless me, how time is running away! I must
be off —"

"Now, Burrowes, don't be in such an
absurd hurry —"

"Hurry! Oh my goodness!" raising his
eyebrows and smiling humourously at Eleanor, "when I've been here an hour and a
quarter by my repeater!—"

"Aye, and don't you often stay gossipping

here an hour and a half by your repeater? Miss Graydon is anxious to say something. Speak out, my dear."

" Mr. Burrowes said just now, sir, that the certificates, to be legal, must be signed by two medical men who had had no previous consultation or meeting. Now, the two men whom the housemaid took to be gentlemen, who called on Miss Clairvaux before she was taken away, and troubled her with impertinent questions, *had* had a previous meeting, for Claudia saw them come up together to the house !"

"That is well suggested, my bright little friend," said Mr. Newland with strong approbation expressed in his face. "You so quietly assume, too, that they *were* medical men, and that Miss Clairvaux *was* taken away. Oh, no apologies, I beg : women have nothing to do with logic, and all to do with affection. You are an excellent partizan."

" Well, sir," said Mr. Burrowes, " I really must be going, so I'll leave you and Miss Graydon together —"

" Stay, stay, stay —"

" I must be going too," said Eleanor rising.

" *Where ?*" said Mr. Newland.

" Ah," said she sadly, " indeed I do not know; since the Peaked House is closed against me. I think I shall return to mamma."

" No, no, no ; a thousand times no !"

" Indeed, sir, I must. I cannot stay here."

" Better go to the Debenhams," interposed Mr. Burrowes.

" The Debenhams are much obliged to you," said Eleanor with spirit. " They would be a little surprised, I think, if I asked them to take me in. I have no claim on them whatever."

" I cannot have you here, you see," said Mr. Newland in his invalid voice, " because my habits —"

"No, sir, thank you."

"Mrs. Burrowes being just confined," said Mr. Burrowes, "makes it awkward, you see, to receive visitors ; but —"

"Thank you very much, but I shall certainly go home.   What can I do here?"

"Do? Everything, my dear young lady," said Mr. Newland, laying his hand on her arm.

"Oh yes ; indeed, Miss Graydon, everything depends on you !"

"How?" said she, amazed.

"Your clear and pointed testimony," said Mr. Newland, "has given us a clue to what seems a nefarious conspiracy. You are the medium through which we hope to obtain access to Mr. Foljambe."

"Yes," said Eleanor, "but I can post my letter in London just as well or better, and get an answer much sooner.   Number 3, Riadore Place," added she, with a little blush and smile, "may not look so impressive at the head of a letter as Stonewall House, but it will answer the purpose just the same."

"Riadore Place, number three," muttered Mr. Newland, making a hasty memorandum. Eleanor could not help thinking. "Here is one by whom all one says is—

'Set in a note-book, conned, and learnt by heart!'"

"But you must communicate with me, my dear."

"Certainly, sir. Riadore Place, Camberwell, will be my address in full." (He booked it.) "And I hope you will direct me what to do next."

"I will. I promise you I will. And you, too must do all you can. Pick up all the information afloat —"

"Ah! Claudia told me there were strange reports in the town. 1 will try to hear something about them before I go away." Mr. Burrowes was now in an agony to be off.

"Shall I leave you here, Miss Graydon?" said he, "or give you a lift towards the town?"

"Give her a lift, by all means," said Mr. Newland. "The day is at its hottest, and the distance a long mile."

"Oh, I think nothing of the walk," said Eleanor, "I would rather ——"

"Nonsense, my good young lady, begging your pardon. Never refuse a good offer. Adieu! be sure you let me hear from you—"

"And what shall you do, sir?" said Mr. Burrowes aside to him,

"I shall write for an expert."

Eleanor did not hear this, or it would have given her pleasure. She did not much like riding in Mr. Burrowes' chaise, for she knew how absurdly censorious some of the townspeople were; and yet, thought she, what need I to care for them? my only care is for Miss Clairvaux. She contented herself with asking him to set her down where he had taken her up, which she said would be a good lift, to which he agreed. So the groom cut across as before. Mr. Newland, having ceremoniously attended her to the door, had retreated before it was opened. John, who performed that office, still looked as if the sky had fallen ; his 'old woman' was viewing the unwonted vision from afar, at the head of the kitchen stairs.

"I got you into the house, you see!" said Mr. Burrowes exultingly as he drove off, "Oh, I can do anything with him! He's a wonderful man! writes like Junius! with equal secrecy, at all events."

Eleanor could hardly help smiling at this, considering how Mr. Burrowes had betrayed the sobriquet of Vindex. And if he could do anything with him, how came it to pass that he had let him shut himself up all these years?

Arrived at the spot where the groom awaited them, she gratefully thanked Mr.

Burrowes for the assistance he had afforded her.

"Oh," said he, " it's all in the day's work. I've given Mr. Newland a new object, and got a woman into the house. Besides, Miss Clairvaux is my neighbour, and has been my patient, and she has plenty of friends as well as enemies, so that one cannot let her drop out of sight without taking some concern in her fate. And, in any way that I can assist you, you may command me; only, you see, my time is pretty much taken up with my practice. Mrs. Burrowes will be about again soon, and then I am sure she will be happy to offer you a bed, or shew you any attention. Good morning, success attend you! you have my hearty good wishes."

And Eleanor again found herself on the high road, in a cloud of dust raised by the retreating wheels. She thought she would call on Hester, and, if she could screw her courage up, on Mrs. Debenham. But this

was a formidable effort to Eleanor, who did
not consider she could claim her friendship
on her own account. Still, the Debenhams
were professed friends of Miss Clairvaux,
whom she was trying to serve.

Hester was her first object. As she
walked along, she thought much of the singular interview she had just taken part in, and
of the sad and strange tale she would have
to relate to her mother when she returned.
How surprised her mother would be to see
her back!—Probably, what a different life
now lay before her, to what she had, a few
hours before, imagined! Poor Miss Clairvaux! where could she be, and how could
they hope to trace her?

Thoughts such as these engaged Eleanor's
mind, till she found herself in the town. On
reaching the greengrocer's, she was disappointed to find that Hester had gone to spend
the day with her family, some miles off, and
consult them what she should do. Eleanor,

therefore, turned towards Mr. Debenham's; but, passing Fidgeon's shop, and remembering that Mr. Horsefield's name was connected with it, she went in and asked for some hair-pins. She was served by a little girl, for Mrs. Fidgeon was so engaged with another customer, that she did not notice Eleanor's entrance. They appeared immersed in gossip, and Eleanor heard her say:

"When a lady like Miss Clairvaux, you know, goes off without paying her bills—"

"How can you say so, Mrs. Fidgeon?" said Eleanor, indignantly. "Miss Clairvaux paid every account as it came in; her butcher, baker, and grocer, every week, her rent every quarter, and her servants' wages to the day. I speak of what I know, for I've seen her do it!"

The two women came to a sudden pause, and exchanged a frightened look. "I beg your pardon, ma'am," said Mrs. Fidgeon, addressing Eleanor in a carefully modulated voice; "but were you attending to what I was saying to my friend?"

"Nobody who came into the shop could help hearing what you were saying, Mrs. Fidgeon; and I think your time might be better employed than in accusing Miss Clairvaux of what she certainly does not deserve."

"Oh, ma'am, I beg your pardon—you're the humble companion, I see. I beg your pardon for not recognizating you before—if you will be so good as to collect yourself, miss, you'll remember I accused Miss Clairvaux of nothing; I was speaking of ladies *like* Miss Clairvaux, and hadn't finished my sentence when you cut me short."

"Ladies who do not pay their bills are *not* like Miss Clairvaux. I shall certainly mention the improper use you have made of her name. I can't think what you meant by it; she certainly owes you nothing."

"I can't say her dealings here have ever been great," said Mrs. Fidgeon, with a toss of the head, "a broom or a blacking-brush, now-and-then; perhaps a sixpenny ball of string. What can I have the pleasure of serving *you* with, miss?"

"Thank you, I only wanted these pins: and have paid for them. Please, Mrs. Fidgeon, refrain from setting idle reports about: when Miss Clairvaux comes home, those who have spread them will look very silly."

"Miss Clairvaux is not likely to come home very soon, ma'am," said Mrs. Fidgeon, with concentrated malice, "leastways, I've been told so."

"By Mr. Horsefield, no doubt," said Eleanor, stoutly.

Mrs. Fidgeon looked confounded.

"I beg your pardon—what name did you say, ma'am?"

"Mr. Horsefield," repeated Eleanor, "I know he comes here, and have seen him."

"I don't know why he shouldn't," put in

Mrs. Fidgeon's ally, coming rather timidly to the rescue.

"No," said Mrs. Fidgeon, rallying, and catching up the word, "I don't know why he shouldn't, for the shop is open to all, and his money is as good as anybody else's, and—"

"And he's a relation besides," put in the ally, mal-adroitly, for which she received a quick look of rebuke.

"That's neither here nor there," said Mrs. Fidgeon, "people are not answerable for their relations."

"No," said Eleanor, "and I don't blame you for being related to him; only you are perhaps aware that he and Miss Clairvaux are not very cordial to one another; he has been sent to her on unpleasant messages sometimes, which have not made her glad to see him; and this may have made her speak to him rather shortly, (for I don't say, Mrs. Fidgeon, that she may not be rather quick-tempered; clever people often are; but she has the best heart!) Mr. Horsefield does not know her as well as I do, and therefore—why, where do you suppose she is now?"

"Ah! miss, no doubt you know better than I do!" said Mrs. Fidgeon with a triumphant look, that said "that was a good stroke of yours, but if you're deep, I am deeper!" Eleanor felt foiled, but did not show it much.

"We had better each attend to our own affairs, I think," said she. "Miss Clairvaux is my dearest friend, and the dear friend of all my family; so you may well suppose we are not going to give her up."

Saying which, she took up her small packet of pins, moved the money towards Mrs. Fidgeon, said "good morning," and quietly quitted the shop, leaving the gossips to ejaculate, "Did you ever?" and "Well I'm sure!" with upraised eyebrows and uplifted hands.

Her heart swelled as she went on her way; she thought "how good Miss Clairvaux had been! how nobly she has behaved! and this is the return." She did not know how much harder it is to escape censure than to gain applause; for this may be won by a single action, whereas that demands that we should never be guilty of a fault or weakness—and, even then, might not let us off.

Before she had gone far, she was descried by Miss Jones, who hastened after her, and laid her hand on her arm.

"My dear Miss Graydon," said she, "this is most fortunate. I have been particularly wishing to see you; about poor Miss Clairvaux, you know, and it won't do to speak of in the middle of the street; besides which, it is coming on to rain, so pray oblige me by stepping into my lodgings which are close by."

Eleanor, inferring from what she said that she had something to communicate about Miss

Clairvaux, immediately complied, and followed her to the side-door (round a corner) of a shop, which admitted them, through a narrow passage, into a dull little parlour, with very meagre pretensions to being well furnished; yet, such as it was, it held all the domestic luxuries that the contented little woman had known for many a year. Her kitten on the rug, her canary in the window, and her knitting on the table, side by side with "Agony Point, or the Groans of Gentility," showed how her time was chiefly spent in-doors; nor was she unhappy.

"I dare say," said she, "this appears to you but a mean abode compared with the refinement you have been accustomed to; but, my dear Miss Graydon, I have long been convinced that one's real satisfactions do not depend on exterior objects, at least in the degree that young people commonly suppose. How glad we all are, for instance, to wear an old shoe!—if we are quite sure nobody will see it;

and there are many other things in the same category with old shoes. When one sits before one's winter fire, in easy shoes, with a good novel to enjoy, and no draught assailing the nape of one's neck, what else do we want? Perhaps you never read novels? I'm sensible they require some excuse—(though *I* read a good many, and find them a cheap substitute for evening society)—but here is one I am now reading, which is not a *mere* novel, but a picture of life and its trials and temptations in the present day. Mrs. Plover insists that it is *real* life, and that Tom Langley is Tom somebody else; and Minnie is I forget who, and the Chesters the Lesters, and Mrs. Stretchem Mrs. Gresham, and so on all through. It may be so, I don't say it isn't, though I don't call it good taste or good feeling (do you?) or even good art, to put such people into a book, unless Queen Elizabeth, you know, and personages of that sort. You and I, my dear, should not like to be put into a book—at least I know I shouldn't; and if authors made a practice of doing such things, they'd be bugbears instead of agreeable lions— and it would shew poverty of imagination, you know, and invention. That's what I always say when Mrs. Plover, or any one says, ' oh, do not read so and so—it shews up the aris- tocracy, and all the characters are from real life.' Why, then, you know, it becomes history —or else slander—and slander I detest, and history I take like medicine, in small doses. At my time of life, one knows pretty well what has happened in former periods ; at least, after going through Russell's Modern Europe, if we remember anything of it—but I dis- tinctly recollect, that when I used to read a daily portion of it to my governess, I used to carry on a separate chain of thought all the time. I read, now, to break my chain of thought, and therefore want something inter- esting enough to fix the attention."

Miss Jones paused for a single instant, and

Eleanor was going to draw her gently to the subject on her thoughts, but the opportunity was not afforded.

"But I really give this writer," resumed Miss Jones, laying her hand on Agony Point, "the credit of not drawing slavishly and satirically from life, but only giving general likenesses, you know, which anybody may do; and oh! how sad it is to read of the troubles of a well-meaning young pair, beginning life together without the least experience, and to feel that they are just the troubles that might occur to any young people in the same position. All the poor young lady's cheeses spoilt, for want of turning and wiping!"

"Just now," said Eleanor, "my thoughts are a good deal diverted from imaginary troubles by real ones. I suppose you have heard of Miss Clairvaux—"

"My dear, my heart really bled for her! If a heart ever really bled, I'm convinced

that mine did. I was quite harrowed—
though that is a strong expression to use,
if one considers what harrowing is—I suppose
you, though a Londoner, may occasionally
have seen a harrow at work—"

"You had something to tell me of her,
I think?"

"I? not a word! I wanted to hear all
about it from you."

"Oh," said Eleanor, in disappointment,
and feeling she was wasting her time, "I
have nothing to say. I only came from
London this morning, and was taken quite
by surprise when I found the house in other
hands."

"It must have been a great shock to you.
And what are you going to do?" said Miss
Jones with lively interest.

"Oh, I shall return home."

"It is quite early yet. Do spend the day
with me!"

"Oh no, thank you; you are very

kind, but I have much to think of and
to do."

"That I can readily believe; but now *do*
take your dinner at my luncheon—I mean
your luncheon at my dinner, for the fact is,
I always dine when other people lunch; much
wholesomer, you know! Now, will you?"

"No, thank you," said Eleanor, "I have
lunched, and—"

"At Mrs. Debenham's?" said Miss Jones,
quickly.

"No," said Eleanor, smiling; "but I am
going there now, as I particularly wish to
see her—"

"She's not at home!"

"Yes, I have been told she returned
yesterday evening."

"How curious! Mrs. Plover called there
yesterday, and asked when she would come
back, and the servant did not seem to have
the least idea. If you have no objection, I
will accompany you."

"Thank you," said Eleanor, "but I do not think that will be a very good plan, because, you see, my time is short, and I want to turn it to account, and I think I can speak more freely to Mrs. Debenhan by myself than with a companion; so that, if you will not be displeased—"

"Not at all—not at all, though I would not have repeated a word! I never do. There's an end of all confidence, you know, when people tell anything. Well, if you really won't stay, all I can say is, I'm very sorry, and I shall be very glad when anything brings you among us again."

And with these and other kind speeches, she allowed Eleanor to leave her.

CHAPTER VI.

People frequently use this expression, " I am inclined
to think so-and-so," not considering that they are then
speaking the most literal of all truths.

Mrs. DEBENHAM was feeding her parrot,
and Mr. Debenham was enjoying the Browbeater, when Eleanor was announced.

" Miss Graydon !" exclaimed he, with a
start of pleasure, " I did not know you had
returned ! How are you? How is Miss
Clairvaux ?"

" Do you not know, then, what has
happened ?" said Eleanor.

"No, indeed," replied he, all alive with curiosity in an instant. "My mother and I have but just come home, and have heard nothing. Pray, put us *au courant*—"

"You look tired, my dear," said Mrs. Debenham, taking her by the hand, and drawing her to the comfortable sofa. "Have a glass of wine."

"O no, ma'am, thank you."

"I am sure you would be better for it. Sam, do see whether the luncheon is removed yet—"

"I have lunched, thank you," said Eleanor; but Mr. Debenham walked off to obey his mother's instructions; and she took advantage of his absence to say in a very friendly manner:

"Is it anything, my dear, that you would rather not say before Sam?"

"Oh no, ma'am, thank you. In fact, I shall be very glad for Mr. Debenham to hear what I have to tell."

He came in as she said this, and imme-diately thought within himself, " some rupture or rumpus with Miss Clairvaux, no doubt; how disagreeable ! I shan't know which side to take."

"Let us hear all about it," said Mrs. Debenham, seating herself beside her, while Mr. Debenham, with a constrained air, took up his position opposite. "I can't think what it can be."

"Perhaps you know," said Eleanor, " that I went to London, about a fortnight ago, to see my mother. I wrote several letters to Miss Clairvaux during my absence; but, to my surprise, received no answers, and this hastened my return. When I came back, I found she was gone !"

" Gone ?" repeated mother and son simul-taneously. Mr. Debenham speaking in a brisk, amused manner.

" And I fear," faltered Eleanor, " she went on compulsion."

" Bless my soul!" exclaimed he, changing
his position very suddenly, and placing himself close to her, "you don't mean to say her
affairs are involved? I should never have
guessed such a thing!"

"Not in the sense in which you use the
word," said Eleanor, and she then related
all that had occurred. They listened with
vivid and painful interest.

"This is probably some dirty contrivance
to compel her to sign," said Mr. Debenham,
"but that a man of Mr. Foljambe's standing
should damage his professional character by
meddling with such work, I really can hardly
believe. Oh, depend on it, it will all be
cleared up."

"But suppose it should not be?"

"Oh, then something must be done."

"What must be done?"

"It must be put into professional hands."

"And that will cost money."

"Certainly it will," said he, smiling.

"I'm sure I don't know where the money is to come from, then," said Eleanor, sighing, "for *we* have very little."

"Dear me, dear me," said Mrs. Debenham, folding her hands.

"Supposing," resumed Eleanor, "that the money were forthcoming, would it be a case in your way?"

"Well, I hardly know," said he, not very encouragingly. "Of course, I could put it in proper train. But counsel must be engaged and so forth."

"My dear, you had better not throw away your money in that way," said Mrs. Debenham. "Law is very expensive, as I, a lawyer's widow and mother, of course know. Suppose Miss Clairvaux should come home to-morrow!"

"Aye, or suppose the sky should fall, mamma," said Mr. Debenham rather disrespectfully. "What we have to suppose is, if she should not. Of course, we should be very glad if she were to walk in upon us ; but her doing so appears unlikely, unless, indeed, she signed the paper, and they let her go."

" I am sure Miss Clairvaux would never sign anything on compulsion," said Eleanor.

" Quite unlikely," repeated he. " Quite unlikely." And he began to play with a paper-knife.

" Very shocking, and very sad," resumed he after a dreary pause. " And what do you mean to do ?"

" Oh, *I* mean to go home again directly, of course." Mr. Debenham looked relieved.

" I have written a note to Mr. Foljambe, which I mean to post in London this evening, if mamma approves it."

" Might I ask what you have written ?"

" You may see it, if you like—if the subject interests you sufficiently." She felt a little wounded by his seeming flagging interest.

" I assure you it does." He read it at-

tentively, and handed it to his mother, observing—

"That will do very well, only you have
not dated it."

"I mean to date it in town. Mr. Newland
said —"

" Mr. Newland !"

" His name escaped me," said Eleanor.

" Do you mean to say you have seen Mr.
Newland ?"

" Yes."

" Of Stonewall ?"

" Yes. He did not wish me to mention it."

" Do you really mean you have bearded
the old lion in his den ?"

" If you like to call him so."

" Well, this is the most wonderfullest
wonder—! You told him all about it ? What
view did he take of it ?"

" He took the most lively interest."

" Well, certainly you are a most courage-
ous young lady," cried Mr. Debenham rub-

bing his hands with glee, and looking at her as if her personal appearance had undergone some remarkable transformation. "Oh, depend upon it, if *he* takes it in hand, all will go right. Old Vindex will make a fine kettle of fish of it. Nothing he'd like better to hold up to the indignation of all mankind than some infringement of the liberty of the British subject.—Well, now, what is he like?"

"Yes, my dear, do tell us what he is like," said Mrs. Debenham.

"He—I really must beg you to excuse me," said Eleanor. "He was most kind and encouraging, but the interview was quite confidential, and he begged me to let him remain out of sight till he was absolutely needed. *Then*, he said, he should not hesitate to come forward."

"Capital," said Mr. Debenham. "Oh, he'll back you up, depend upon it."

"But let me beg you, for Miss Clairvaux's

sake," said Eleanor earnestly, " to comply with my request not to mention his name at present —"

" Of course—of course."

" Of course, my dear," said Mrs. Debenham. " Professional people are upon honour. And I never divulge anything."

" Well, and so... What did the old gentleman say? He who declared a petticoat should never enter his house! How did he look when you first went in ?"

Mr. Debenham was here summoned away to see some one on business.

" Don't go till I come back," said he hastily.

" I believe I must," said Eleanor, " for the train —"

" 4.30 ! Don't go before the 4.30 !" and he hastened away. How much more interested in the case he appeared, now that he knew an influential man was interested in it !

" I hardly know what to say about staying," said Eleanor wearily, " for I have had much to fatigue me, and have hardly any strength left."

"My dear, you shall lie down on the sofa," said Mrs. Debenham, "and remain quite quiet. I will draw down the blinds, and then you will very likely get a little nap. There's the visitors' bell! Never mind—I will shut the folding-doors, and receive whoever it is in the front drawing-room, and nobody will know you are in here."

She vanished as she spoke, closing the folding-doors after her, and Eleanor was very glad to take off her bonnet, lie down, and close her eyes. She could not sleep, however. She could hear the servant announce Mrs. Plover; and, the next instant, the treacherous folding-door, not having been bolted, parted company with its fellow, which creaked and gaped a little, so as to admit the voices; but as Eleanor concluded it to be only a common morning visit, and knew she could not be seen where she was, but thought she might be if she rose to close the door, she did not move.

Ordinary inquiries about each other's health were followed by seaside details of a commonplace kind, which seemed not without their acceptance, however, to Mrs. Plover. She then gave the dialogue a violent wrench, by saying :

" Well, I suppose you have heard what has happened here, in your absence ?"

" What, about poor Miss Clairvaux ?" said Mrs. Debenham.

" My dear Mrs. Debenham, don't waste your pity on that woman ! If ever a creature deserved to have her pride taken down, she did !"

" What, for a natural infirmity, maybe," said Mrs. Debenham.

" Oho, that's the side you take, is it ! Well, it's my side, too. Yes, I believe a person never *could* have gone on so, if she had been all right !"

"But, 'gone on'? How?" said Mrs. Debenham. "I did not know she had gone on in any particular manner—"

" Oh, you don't hear these things as I do—they're all brought to me! A little bird in the air tells me everything! Nothing escapes me."

"Well, but Miss Clairvaux?—"

"Miss Clairvaux has been going on for a long time as nobody else would. Think of her fraternizing with the equestrian troop, inviting the clown to dine with her on a roast loin of pork, making up a bed for him in her scullery, and telling him she should like to establish him in a turnpike, or gentleman's lodge!"

" No, no, no," said Mrs. Debenham gently. " I can't believe it."

" But you may, for it's every word true! I've had it from the best authority. Oh, it's incredible the fancy she conceived for those Dicks, the very worst family in the parish, all for the sake of that clown! why, she went over to the Union, to see old Dick in the infirmary, supplied him with money against the rules, and actually kissed him!"

"Kissed that dirty old man? oh, I really *cannot* believe that," said Mrs. Debenham laughing.

"Just tell me," said Mrs. Plover excitedly, "whether you would decide that a person who could do such things *must* be a little cracked."

"Well, I think I may allow that. Yes, I do."

"Then, I'm quite satisfied," cried Mrs. Plover, "because it is actual fact."

"But why should it satisfy you," interposed Mrs. Debenham, "to prove poor Miss Clairvaux deranged? what satisfaction would there be in that?"

"Oh, there's always satisfaction in proving one is right."

"Well, poor lady, I wish her well out of her troubles, I'm sure," said Mrs. Debenham, "for she is a great favourite of ours, though we have not seen as much of her as we could wish. *Where* is she, did you say?"

"That's not exactly known—that is, it is not talked about," said Mrs. Plover. "Of course, the proper parties know it."

"Who are the proper parties?"

"I don't feel that I am quite authorized to name names," said Mrs. Plover. "But, my dear Mrs. Debenham, what an awful thing for her to be driven screaming through the streets!"

"*Was* she?" cried Mrs. Debenham in alarm.

"Crying 'help! help!'"

"Why did nobody help her?"

"It was nobody's place, you know, to interfere."

"Dear me, I think it was everybody's place to interfere," said Mrs. Debenham. "If I had been a man, I'm sure I should. I can't bear the idea of a woman being snatched from her home in broad daylight, and carried off screaming, because it was nobody's business to interfere ! Why, the whole town ought to have risen *en masse !* I shall tell Sam of it, directly he comes in, and I'm sure he'll make a stir."

"Ah, I incline to believe no stir can be made now," said Mrs. Plover, "for she's safely caged somewhere, and nobody knows where."

"I'm certain it can be made," said Mrs. Debenham, "by *habeas corpus*, or something of that sort, or England can't be England. Dear me, why if only the people that Miss Clairvaux had helped in their deep affliction, had but rallied round her, the thing could not have happened. There'll be something upon it in the Browbeater, you may depend."

"Perhaps Mr. Debenham writes for the Browbeater," said Mrs. Plover, with a little sarcasm.

"No, he does not, though he is quite

capable of it. I should not be surprised if it were to get into the Times. And then we shall all figure before the public, those that had any hand in it. I'm very glad I was away."

"Oh, we should all have been very glad of that," said Mrs. Plover, though she never spoke a falser word. "Well, good morning; I'm delighted to find you so well."

When Mrs. Debenham returned to the back drawing-room, she found Eleanor looking much distressed.

"I'm afraid you did not get much rest, my dear," said she.

"No," said Eleanor, "the door opened a little, so that I could not help hearing every word. What cruel things she said! How kind you were, Mrs. Debenham! I can assure you, Miss Clairvaux never dined with the clown—"

"My dear, it would be an insult to her to suppose it for an instant. A pretty thing for Miss Clairvaux to do, so proud as she is, according to Mrs. Plover."

Mr. Debenham here came in.

"What! going away, Miss Graydon?" said he. "I am glad you have awaited my return, at all events. I wish you were not going away at all. Mother, could not you give Miss Graydon a bed, do you think?"

"Certainly, and with much pleasure," said Mrs. Debenham, "I was thinking of it just before you spoke."

"Thank you very much," said Eleanor, "but I really must go to mamma. Much may depend on it."

"And much may depend on your remaining here, and watching Miss Clairvaux's interests. Indeed, Miss Graydon, the best thing you can do, when you have seen Mrs. Graydon, and given Mr. Foljambe time to answer your letter, will be to come back to us; for nothing effectual will be done without you. Burrowes says so; I've been talking to Burrowes; Burrowes says it's wonderful how you stirred up old Vindex. So, directly you get in a fix in town, come down and try to set things moving here. I shall he honoured and delighted, and I am sure my mother will be the same."

"Oh yes, indeed!" said Mrs. Debenham. Eleanor thanked her very warmly, and said that if circumstances rendered it advisable, she would gratefully avail herself of their kindness.

So then Mr. Debenham insisted on accompanying her to the station. He knew, though she did not, what construction would be put by the gossips on his "philandering" a young lady through the streets; therefore, it was magnanimous of him to brave it; but he had caught a little moral courage from her and from Mr. Newland. He looked about him, nodded here, nodded there, but in a grave manner, as much as to say, 'I've a great deal on my mind—these are troublous times.' And when he parted with her on the platform, it was with deferential politeness.

Soon Eleanor was whirling towards London, hurrying along the platform, and rattling in a cab to Riadore Place. Mrs. Graydon's surprise at her appearance almost took away her breath.

" My dear love, what's the matter? *You* are alive and well, I am thankful to see ; but what has happened ?"

George fortunately was at home ; so Eleanor could tell her story to both at once. After a rapid and agitating debate, the letter to Mr. Foljambe was dated and posted. After this, they resumed their conversation, and did not break it off till midnight.

What an unexpectedly eventful, painful day it had been ! Eleanor felt as if nothing would still the tremor of her nerves ; and yet she was so tired, and there was something so sweet in lying down beside her own dear

mother, whose very presence seemed a safeguard, that she no sooner closed her eyes than
she was overcome by deep, dreamless sleep,
like a little bird under the maternal wing.

CHAPTER VII.

Economy is no disgrace : it is better to be living on a
little, than outliving a great deal.

ELEANOR's memory, assisted by a directory,
had supplied her with Mr. Foljambe's address ;
but three days passed and no notice was taken
of the letter. The suspense was most trying.
At Mrs. Graydon's suggestion, George called
at Mr. Foljambe's chambers, to ask if he were
within. "Not in town," was the disappointing answer.

Nevertheless, Mrs. Graydon would not be
foiled by it. She made inquiries of a char-

woman, technically called "bedmaker," who was clearing the door-step of the next house, and learnt of her that Mr. Foljambe certainly *was* in town; she had seen him that morning. Yet his office-door was locked, a card with "out of town" was wafered on it, and nobody answered the bell when she rang it. No progress was made.

The afternoon post brought Eleanor a missive which made her cheeks burn. Her letters to Miss Clairvaux, opened, smoothed out, folded lengthways one over another, made up into a book-post parcel open at the ends, tied most carelessly with a piece of string passed once round, and directed to her in a vulgar, sprawling hand. On the first page of the first letter, the impudent interlineation of "with Mr. Horsefield's comp^s." The low fellow had evidently read them, and did not take the trouble to conceal it! The cover was stamped 'Meadowleigh.'

Though she took it for granted at first, that this proved her letter to Mr. Foljambe had been received and acted on, this by no means followed. Mr. Horsefield might have access to the Peaked House, find the letters there, take possession of them, keep them as long as he liked, and finally send them back, solely on his own insolent account. It was just what one might expect of him. Eleanor wrote to Mr. Newland that she had had no answer from Mr. Foljambe, and could not learn where he was.

In the evening, George burst into the room in which she and her mother were sitting, looking brimful of intelligence.

" We've traced her at last!" said he, rubbing his hands. " Some fellow-students and I have been hard at it for days; and now we know where she is!"

" Oh, I'm so thankful! Where?"

" In a private asylum of very indifferent reputation near Narrowgate."

" Can we get at her ?"

" I'm afraid not."

" How dare they keep her there ?"

" They say, of course, she requires treatment. They've had the proper forms made
out, so no one could hinder them."

" How did your friends find her out ?"

" One of them (not much of a gentleman)
is related to a practitioner, still less of a gentleman, who happens to be medical officer of
this particular asylum. He *ought* to be resident
in it, but is not ; and he admits that he filled
up the statement after one very cursory observation."

" What statement ?"

" A statement (properly speaking, made by
a resident officer), of the mental and bodily
condition of the patient, not less than two
days after the date of his or her admission.
This delay is intended to give time for due
examination of the case ; but Quarridge owns he
signed it sooner, after seeing her only once."

"Did he tell you so?"

"No, I have not seen him. Of course he would not commit himself so to a stranger. He told his cousin, Kit Quarridge, who pumped it out of him. The place is far down in the country—I had to pay Kit's expenses."

"That was very kind of you, George!"

"Well, you know the old lady was very kind to *me*, and one good turn deserves another."

"I wonder if I could get admission to her," said Eleanor, eagerly.

"Of course not; you must not think of it. We want to get her out—not you in. Keep outside, Nelly, as long as you can."

"But, just to speak one little word of comfort—give her one kiss!—"

"They wouldn't let you, I tell you; they've put her in the seclusion ward."

"That means, in solitary confinement," ejaculated Mrs. Graydon. "Dreadful!"

"Well, mother, don't make the worst of

it. Miss Clairvaux has lived in voluntary seclusion for years; and, I'll answer for it, would tell you, if you asked her, that she preferred her own company to that of the inmates of the asylum."

"It is very sad, either way," said Mrs. Graydon, wiping away a tear.

"Sad, even if it were needful," said Eleanor, "but, when it is *not*, it is scandalous."

"Do you know what account the doctor gave in his report?"

"Quarridge told all about it. Mr. Foljambe had got a keeper from the asylum to go with him in a fly to Meadowleigh. . . . Kit was obliged to go very cautiously to work, to get it out of him, I assure you. Oh, he was as sly as a fox. He went down there with a return-ticket, called on his cousin, and pretended his object was to see whether there was an opening there for another practitioner. Quarridge assured him there was not; however, he was very civil to him and asked him to dinner; and as Quarridge has married his cook, you may depend on it the dinner was a good one. After dinner they had spirits-and-water. Kit told some of his funny hospital stories; and Quarridge, not to be behindhand, capped them with some of his asylum stories. Miss Clairvaux's name came out quite naturally, without Kit's showing the least interest in it. And so Quarridge went on to tell what fight she had made, how she had struggled and cried out, and what means they took to quiet her."

"What were those means?" said Mrs. Graydon, anxiously.

"That's neither here nor there," said George. "Some of these days, she may tell you herself. Quarridge had nothing to do with that though, you know; he did not see her till she was in the asylum. He made his first inspection of her through a small sliding pannel—thought she looked like Niobe."

" Well ?"

" When he went in, she looked haughty
enough, but said quite quietly, 'May I ask
why I am placed here, and how long I am
to stay?' Quarridge could see nothing the
matter with her; nothing to report; so he
says he was obliged to put her up a little.
And then, to use his own words, there was
old gooseberry to pay."

" George, I must write of this to Mr.
Newland!" exclaimed Eleanor.

" You must be quick, then, or you'll lose
the post."

Her pen flew over the paper, and he
rushed off with the note directly it was
finished.

" I have not told him half," said Eleanor,
regretfully, " and I fear I expressed myself
very incoherently. It would, perhaps, be best
to go down to him."

" Only it costs so much money, my dear,"
said Mrs. Graydon. " I have very little in

hand for extras. However, there are two or three more of your papa's sketches that we could sell, and I would readily do so to help Miss Clairvaux. Only we must not rush into needless expenses."

"Certainly not," said Eleanor; and she began to think how she could turn her talents to account. Her mind was not composed enough for authorship; so she set about copying one of her father's water-colour landscapes; and felt the calming influence of her employment.

"Eleanor! that sky is excellent," said her mother. "Be careful of the middle-distance. Perhaps, by selling your copy, we may be able to retain the original."

Encouraged by these words, Eleanor painted all day. When she had dusted their little sitting-room, there was no other in-door employment for her; for Mrs. Graydon, assisted by a little girl, did all that their small household required. Nor had she any temptation to go out. The heat was fierce, and when the windows were opened they admitted nothing but dust. How different from the breezy air, scented with heath flowers, that freshened her at the Peaked House! But if she missed it, how must Miss Clairvaux do so? That thought was enough to still any murmur.

By return of post, she heard from Mr. Newland. He wrote,

"My dear young lady,

"Your news is of the utmost importance; but disjointed. I fancy you have, in your haste, left out something. Could you run down here again? What you have already done surprises me.

"Your faithful servant,

"VALENTINE NEWLAND."

"We must go together then," said Mrs. Graydon. "I cannot have you flying about

the country by yourself, even for Miss Clairvaux. You have finished your drawing, so
I will take it and the original into the Strand,
and if yours will not fetch enough, I will sell
both."

"But, mamma, second-class return-tickets
will not cost very much."

"I don't know that I shall take return-
tickets. We may find it needful to remain at
Meadowleigh for a few days; and you and I
shall only require a bedroom."

Mrs. Graydon returned with five pounds
in her purse, greatly elated at her success.
She then arranged everything as well as she
could for George's comfort, devolving great
responsibilities on the little maid with the
grey head on green shoulders, who was suit-
ably impressed with the importance of her
position; and then, having each a little leather
bag packed as tight as it could hold, the
mother and daughter started on their journey,
accompanied by George to the station.

It really was very delightful to Eleanor to find herself travelling with her mother; and any change was such a novelty to Mrs. Graydon that she was fully alive to all the agreeable features of the jaunt, letting nothing escape her keen observation on the road.

"If I were rich, I believe I should be very fond of travelling," said she smiling. "I have always enjoyed getting out of town, even as far as Hendon. Directly I have seen the purple mallows at the roadside, I have felt myself in the country."

A cynical-looking fellow-passenger apparently sleeping, furtively opened one eye, and gave her a contemptuous glance with it, that plainly said 'what a cockney!' She did not see it, and continued to Eleanor:

"For my own part, I should like to be going a hundred miles instead of thirty. How little I knew, when I woke, this morning, where I was going! As ignorant of

what was about to happen as poor Miss
Cl...."

A warning look from Eleanor prevented
the mention of the name. It is very unsafe
to talk of private affairs in railway carriages.
Their fellow-traveller was attending to every
word; possibly only out of idle curiosity, but
how could they tell that? Eleanor remembered
the rebuke of the Quaker to the young officer
in the Spectator: "Why didst thou fleer
at our friend, who feigned himself asleep? He
said nothing; but how dost thou know what
he containeth?" and she also remembered
how she had been startled on her first journey
to Meadowleigh, by the mention of Miss
Clairvaux's name, coupled with small-talk
about her going to bed early, and how odd
Mr. Debenham looked when he found her
to be Miss Clairvaux's guest.

That remembrance brought with it a train
of others—the midnight alarm of fire—Toby's
leap from the window with his father on his

back—Miss Clairvaux's ministrations—her exceeding tenderness towards the poor—her bluntness to the upper classes: harmless eccentricities as Eleanor had at the time deemed them, that were now bringing condign punishment on her. Truly, it was an awful warning not to be eccentric.

Still, in every coterie, one notices so many peculiar people and peculiar ways, that Eleanor wondered Miss Clairvaux's peculiarities should be visited on her so heavily, till she remembered that she had always rowed against the stream. Not content with doing what she considered right herself, she openly condemned those whom she thought doing wrong; and this made them smart. Hence, she was not a popular person; though there were many by whom she was valued, and some by whom she was gratefully loved.

On reaching the Meadowleigh station, Eleanor persuaded her mother to engage the little poney carriage which happened to be waiting, "for," said she, "it is a long mile to Stonewall, in the full glare of the sun, and we may as well be cool when we get there," to which Mrs. Graydon agreed.

Mr. Newland was awaiting them in full toilette, for he was very sensitive as to his appearance before women ; and this, coupled with the indolence that had crept on him, was the chief reason of his rigorous exclusion of the fair sex from his presence.

"Welcome, welcome, young lady," said he, half rising to receive her. "I expected this—what! another lady too? Your good mother, no doubt, though at present I do not trace any likeness."

"I hope, sir, you will excuse my accompanying my daughter," said Mrs. Graydon, rather awe-stricken.

"Madam, you have done quite right. Though Miss Graydon is a miracle of discretion, she is too young and pretty to fly about

the world by herself. And now, we will
have something to eat —"

He offered his arm to Mrs. Graydon with
grave courtesy, and led the way to the dining-
room, Eleanor closing the procession.

"Burrowes was to have been here," said
Mr. Newland, as he cut up a stuffed fowl
with majestic deliberation, "but Burrowes is
unpunctual. I never wait for him, especially
when not quite well, and I have been very
poorly lately—very poorly."

On this, Mrs. Graydon made special inquiries as to his ailments, a subject on which
he seemed glad to dilate ; for with occasional
digressions, the subject lasted during the
course of a very excellent meal.

"Burrowes won't come to-day," said he,
at its end, "it's no good waiting for Burrowes, so we'll proceed to business. My
good young lady, you sent me most important news yesterday, but there was one part
of it I could neither make head nor tail

of. Oblige me by looking through your letter."

He handed it to her, and Eleanor, hastily glancing over it, blushed to see she had omitted an important word, so as to render the sentence nonsense.

She corrected the mistake, and excused herself by saying, " I wrote in such haste to save the post that I hardly knew what I said."

" Ah, that's generally the case with ladies," said Mr. Newland, smiling. " Do not think, however, that I confound you with the common herd. You have great sense. It is wonderful how you have ferretted out Miss Clairvaux. We were quite at fault."

" It was through my brother, sir. What is to be done next ?"

" We shall see, we shall see. You remember my saying, at our former interview, that two things required to be ascertained —first, whether Miss Clairvaux were under

restraint ; second, whether she required to be
so ?"

" Yes, sir."

" Well, you and your brother have found
out the first. It remains to discover the
second."

" It seems to me to be clear as day," said
Eleanor, quickly.

" Ah, young ladies jump very briskly to
conclusions sometimes, by virtue of that
quality called intuition, which Providence has
given them instead of judgment. I don't
undervalue it, by any means. Let me give
you some strawberries. You prefer cherries ?
they are not so wholesome, you know. Young
people, Mrs. Graydon, don't care for what is
wholesome. You and I prefer strawberries."

He bruised his strawberries, adding wine
and sugar, in a meditative way; and presently
said :

" Cheshire. We must get somebody to go
to Cheshire. It was in Cheshire that Mr.

Clairvaux was 'found drowned.' We must try to rummage up all about it."

" I will undertake that, if you like, sir," said Mrs. Graydon with vivacity. " I should very likely find out more than any one else would."

" My good madam, you delight me !" said he, stretching out his hand to her and grasping hers cordially. " You will be ten thousand times better than a man. Go down to the village (you know the name, Miss Graydon ? no ? hum, that is awkward—")

"Never mind, sir," said Mrs. Graydon, " I shall be sure to find it—if I don't in one place I'll go to another; examine the tombstones, talk to the sextons and so forth."

" Excellent, excellent," said he. " As is the daughter, so is the mother. Why, Cheshire is not such an enormous county, after all ! you'll be able to go through the length and breadth of it in a month."

" A month, sir ?" exclaimed Mrs. Graydon,

" I shall have come to the end of my money before that."

" Money must be no object," replied he, " money must be no object. The affair now passes from Miss Graydon's hands into mine. She did what I could not do, and found the clue; I do what she cannot do, and find the money. 'Tis quite simple, each does what he best can."

Taking a twenty-pound note from his pocket-book, he gave it to her, saying,

" This is on Miss Clairvaux's account. You employ it in her interest. If more is wanting, you will let me know."

" Thank you, sir, I am sure this will be more than enough."

" I hope you mean me to go with you, mamma," said Eleanor.

" No, my dear, it would needlessly increase the expense."

" And decrease the chances of success," said Mr. Newland. " A quiet little lady like

Mrs. Graydon may go hither and thither, in and out; asking a question here, a question there, and excite no notice. Add a young lady to the party, and the whole case is altered. Besides, you are wanted here: we cannot spare you."

" But how can I stay here, without mamma?" said Eleanor, looking distressed.

" Mrs. Debenham, my dear," suggested Mrs. Graydon. But Eleanor looked rather reluctant.

" We really cannot spare you," urged Mr. Newland. " You are the only one who can supply missing links. The whole case may be spoilt by your being at a distance."

" Sooner than that should be, sir, I will go to Mrs. Debenham, if she will have me—"

" That's right: I know she will have you; I said so yesterday. I said to Burrowes, ' my note will bring Miss Graydon down to us: when we get her, we must not let her go away.' 'No,' said he, 'she can go to the Debenhams, for the Debenhams are anxious to have her—Mrs. Debenham told me so herself.' "

Eleanor could not help smiling at this fresh proof of the man, supposed to know nothing, knowing all the small talk of the place.

" Well, then, sir," said she, " I will stay there till I hear from mamma."

" Till your mamma returns—"

" No, I don't say that ; but till I hear from her."

"Employ your time well, then, in the interim, and don't go away without letting me know."

" How shall I employ my time ?"

" By collecting whatever evidence may prove serviceable to your friend, and communicating it to me. I shall put it into shape, and place it in proper hands."

" Have you an atlas, or gazetteer, sir ?"

"Both. Do you want to look into them ?"

"Yes, to see about Cheshire."

They returned to the study, and he placed the atlas and gazetteer before her. She opened one and her mother the other.

"Oh, mamma! what a long journey! Chester is a hundred and eighty-two miles from London."

"Yes, dear, but we are thirty miles on the road already; and you know, I said this morning, how I should enjoy a long journey. Cheshire is not altogether an unknown county to me. I stayed there when I was a girl, in an old farm-house: perhaps the people belonging to it are still living. At any rate, it will be very pleasant to inquire, and give me an ostensible object."

"Capital, capital!" said Mr. Newland. "You two deserve, one as much as the other, to be entitled helpmeets for man."

When they had gleaned all that the atlas,

gazetteer, and railway-guide could tell them, they took leave of Mr. Newland, and drove back to the station.

CHAPTER VIII.

But who is this? what thing of sea or land?

ELEANOR having seen her mother off in the train, left the station and took the road to the town. There was nearly half a mile to walk along a straight road. Had she consulted her own inclinations, she would not have sought Mrs. Debenham's hospitality ; but she felt herself now embarked in a grave enterprise, from whence it would be cowardly and selfish to draw back.

How singular that her mother's devotion

to another's interests should actually have procured her a treat exactly suited to her mind! She had often heard her express a wish to revisit the scenes of her childhood, and ascertain whether her early friends were yet alive.

As Eleanor walked onward, she saw a solitary figure approaching her from the town. It did not strike her that it was any one she knew; yet, as the figure approached her nearer and nearer, something in the general mien seemed familiar to her, and she was unable to help feeling strangely anxious to see whether the face bore a corresponding resemblance. The pedestrian was a light, active young man, brown as an olive, except where his hat shaded his open brow; with good black eyes, dark curly hair, and white teeth gleaming when he smiled, above a short curly beard and beneath a dark moustache. His dress was singular and picturesque. As they drew closer to one another, she slackened her pace, and he quickened his, almost into a run. It was Maurice Day!

"Oh, Maurice!" exclaimed she, as he took both her hands in his, and kissed her. It was the first time he had ever done so; but that interchanged look had so instantaneously convinced each of the other's good faith, that the impulse to set this seal to it was irresistible.

"Oh, Maurice! how came you here?"

"To seek you out, of course!"

"How could you know I was here?"

"How? Why, through Sophy, to be sure! That abominable sister of mine, I found, would have made mischief between us —"

"Oh! no; she could not —"

"I'm glad to hear you say so; for, indeed, Eleanor, that letter of yours to her made me think you were very near giving me up."

Eleanor blushed deeply.

"Sophy should never have shown you that letter," said she.

"Oh, I took it," said he mischievously. "What! do you think I could see a missive in your handwriting and not make prize of it? Oh, we had a regular struggle, I snatched it, held it out of her reach, she laughed, cried 'you'd better not.' I, like a fool as I was, thought it must contain something very sweet about my charming self— read it—found everything on the wrong tack—was served right."

"Indeed I think so," said Eleanor laughing.

"But why, in the name of patience, should Sophy interfere between us? She likes you —loves me. Why should she set us at cross-purposes?"

"She wanted to reserve you for a Countess, I believe."

"Countess—fiddlestick! There's no Italian countess that has crossed my path, that could tempt me to swerve from *you*, Eleanor, even in a passing thought! No, I've been as true to you as Leander to Hero, or Romeo to Juliet, or any other faithful lover in story or history! However, I thank Sophy for having brewed this little storm; because it sent me over here as fast as the railroad could carry me, and procured me this blissful, blessed meeting."

"As fast as the railroad could carry you! Why, my letter to Sophy was written weeks ago."

"But I never saw it till last week—I had been dodging the malaria at Palestrina and Poli. Directly I knew what mischief she had done, I started off; nothing could keep me!"

"Have you not taken rather an unadvised step?"

. "Supposing I have, who can blame me? Oh, unadvised enough! Sophy's advice would have been quite the other way."

" Please don't be hard upon Sophy."

" Well, I'll tell you what Sophy has done
for herself—she won't care much whether I'm
hard or soft, for she's going to set up house-
keeping on her own account. She has gone
and engaged herself to a Sardinian officer."

"Dear me, I'm very glad—that is, if he's
a nice man."

" Oh, he's well enough—wears moustaches
as long as Victor Emmanuel's. He will carry
her off to Turin when I get back."

" But shall not you miss her very much?"

" Oh no! I mean to have another house-
keeper soon."

" Who?" said Eleanor.

" Why you, to be sure," said he, laughing.
" I don't mean to wait for you a day longer
than I can help it. Meanwhile, how are you
getting along with Miss Clairvaux? Does
the old lady continue kind to you?"

" Oh, Maurice, I'm not with Miss Clairvaux now!"

"Indeed!" exclaimed he with some surprise. "Then how come you here?"

"Something very sad has happened. I
am here on Miss Clairvaux's affairs. It is
a long story—"

"Suppose then, Eleanor, we turn about,
and go to the railway station. Nobody will
be there, unless a porter or two, till the next
train comes in. There you can tell me the
long story."

"Well, I think it would be very shady and
pleasant, sitting on the bench on the platform."

That the story did not seem long to
Maurice, sitting on the bench in the pleasant
shade with her he most loved, can surprise
no one. Much conversation about it of course
ensued.

"Well," said he, "I don't half like your
putting up at this Mr. Debenham's, because,
you see, I've not the privilege of the entrée;
however, I shall 'take mine ease at

mine inn,' where I have already left my bag."

"Oh, I don't think that would be a very good plan."

"Why not?"

"I don't think mamma would like it— people talk so."

"What is there to talk about, in an artist staying at a country inn? I shall go out sketching; unless I can take part in this business of yours. Is there any way in which I can help you?"

"None that I know of, thank you. . . . . Oh, indeed, Maurice, I think you ought to go away!"

"Where to?"

"To Rome."

"You seem particulary anxious to get rid of me, I think!"

"You know it is not that; only—"

"How do I know it is not that? Oh, I begin to have my suspicions about this Mr.

Debenham. I shall look him up—perhaps pick a quarrel with him."

" Now, Maurice!—"

" Well, I won't tease you any more, though it's very delightful. Don't go yet."

" It is time for me to go to Mrs. Debenham."

" Then I'll attend you there."

" Only to the beginning of the town, please."

" Very well; only to the beginning of the town. Anything to please my sweet Eleanor."

Of course, luck would have it, that before they reached the beginning of the town, Mr. Burrowes drove past them, looked hard at Maurice in his knickerbockers and coloured stockings, and then with an expressive smile at Eleanor, who felt silly enough, and said to her companion :

" It was too bad of you to make yourself so conspicuous. I am almost ashamed of being seen walking with you."

"What do you call conspicuous?" said he, unconcernedly, taking off his brown felt hat with its broad flap, and twirling it round. "Is it my sombrero? You can't think how comfortable it is. Parasol and umbrella at once! Or do my knickerbockers, or violet stockings, or buskins offend your fastidiosity? Oh, artists always wear these things when they're out pleasuring. You should see them at Bettws-y-Cred!"

"Only, this is not Bettws-y-Cred, and you will make people stare."

"Let them stare, and welcome. Perhaps it may bring grist to my mill. 'Who is that distinguished-looking young man?' 'Oh, he's a distinguished artist from Rome.' 'Is he capable, do you think, of undertaking a five hundred pound commission or two? I want one or two history pieces for my gallery.' 'Oh, I should say he's quite capable—he looks it!'"

"Maurice, you conceited creature! There

are no people hereabouts, I can tell you, capable of giving five hundred pound commissions; unless Mr. Newland, whose means are best known to himself."

"Direct me to Mr. Newland. I'll plant my little tent in front of his window, and begin sketching the house."

"But there's nothing to sketch. It is surrounded by a high stone wall, which gives it its name. The wall reaches half way up the first floor windows."

"Then I'll sketch the wall. 'Here, gentlemen and ladies, you see Mr. Newland's house, he must either be in it or out of it.' Or what think you of my taking your public hall, and putting up a placard, 'On view, Stonewall, the seat of the celebrated Blank Newland, Esquire, with Mr. Newland himself inside. Admission, one shilling!'"

"Too cheap," said Eleanor, laughing. "'Too cheap to pay the expenses of the hall, if there were one, considering the number of visitors you would have."

" What ! wouldn't he draw ? I thought he would draw."

" Well, perhaps he would, more than anybody else in the neighbourhood, for all are very desirous to see him.   Only, according to your plan, they would not see him after all !"

" Don't you know the story about the country gentleman who employed an artist to paint Pharaoh and his host drowned in the Red Sea ? The painter did his best for the subject; but when his patron came to look at it, he said, ' But Mr. So-and-so, Pharaoh does not look *in* the sea, he only looks *near* it.'   On this, the artist threw a little more force into the background, which seemed to make the figures retire a little more, but still the same objection was made, ' they only seem *near* the sea, they don't seem *in* it.'   At last, tired by ineffectual efforts to satisfy the captious critic, he painted the picture entirely

out with Indian red and sent it home. The
ignorant party was completely satisfied!
and often, when doing the honours of his
gallery to his friends, he would say, 'Here,
you see, is a picture of Pharaoh and his host
drowned in the Red Sea.' 'But Mr. So-and-
so,' they would object, 'we don't see the host,
nor Pharaoh either.' 'Oh, they're all there
safe enough,' he would reply, 'I saw them
first at the water's edge, then a little way
in, then a little farther, so that I know they
are now completely in.' "

Eleanor laughed, though she had heard the
story before. "Who was that queer little
body," said Maurice, stopping short, "who
looked so hard at us as she passed?"

"I did not observe," said Eleanor, glancing
round. "Oh, it is Miss Jones! what a
pity! she will say all sorts of things."

"What *can* she say? What care I for
Miss Jones or Miss Bones? That name would
suit her best, I think."

" Come, Maurice, we must part now. Good morning."

" 'Good morning,' indeed, just as if we saw each other every day? A pretty leave taking of a fellow from the banks of the Tiber! I don't believe you are any more glad to see me than the Elector of Saxony was to see Charles the Twelfth, when he called on him at Dresden. Well, there must be no kissing on the Queen's highway, I suppose, with Miss Bones turning round to stare, so I'll only treat her to a little dumb shew."

The thoughtless young artist threw himself into one or two exaggerated attitudes, raised his sombrero high in air, clapped his hand to his forehead, and then turned off as if in the depths of desperation. He turned round, about fifty yards off, to do it again; but Eleanor was walking swiftly from him in another direction, and only Miss Jones was watching him by stealth (having walked slowly back for that purpose) so he only gave his forehead another bang, and hurried impetuously into the town.

"Was there ever anything like that!" thought Miss Jones. "I would not have missed it for the world. What an extraordinarily dressed young man! So handsome, too! What an agonizing leave-taking! How one would like to know the rights of it. Miss Graydon must either be in a dreadful state of mind, or most unfeeling. I wonder which. How came she to be down here again; and where is he staying? I shall soon ascertain."

Meanwhile, Eleanor, provoked, and yet amused with Maurice, and inexpressibly delighted and comforted by his unexpected reappearance, was walking rapidly towards Mrs. Debenham's; breathing voiceless thanksgivings for having found that a good understanding existed between them. Her inmost heart was bound up in his; the thought of his inconstancy had pained her on his account almost as much as her own—it seemed so to lower his character! But it was all cleared up! there was not a shadow between them. All they had to do was to wait; and that she could do, as she had hitherto done, contentedly, hopefully, gratefully.

When she met Mrs. Debenham, her face looked so relieved from care, her eyes were so bright with hidden happiness, that the kind old lady said,

"Miss Graydon, you have heard good news, I'm sure! I can see it."

"Yes," said Eleanor, calming herself, "I unexpectedly met an old friend just now, which gave me pleasure; but I have no good news to tell of Miss Clairvaux, for our fears are realized, she is in confinement!"

"Ah, we have heard that sad news already," said Mrs. Debenham. "Mr. Newland communicated it to Mr. Burrowes, who had his permission to tell it to Sam; not a creature besides has heard a word of it, I assure you, unless from some other source. But some other informant certainly has been at work, because every tradesman in the place knows something about it—"

"Through Mr. Horsefield, it must be, then," said Eleanor. "Is he down here still?"

"No. I heard he went away in a second-class carriage, yesterday; but he flies up and down when it suits him."

"Mrs. Debenham, you were kind enough, the last time I was here, to say—"

"That I would give you a bed? My dear, the little blue room is quite ready for you. I have just been setting some roses and mignionette in the little glass in the toilette-pin-cushion. Mr. Newland said, through Mr. Burrowes, that he expected you down, and that we might expect to see you. How curious, that that old gentleman, never seen, and hitherto supposed so misanthropical and valetudinarian, should be regulating even the smallest details of this affair! It seems that he has an extraordinary opinion of Miss Clairvaux; has known all about the good she has done in the neighbourhood; has been particularly struck at its having been effected with so little money; has especially been pleased with her independence, simplicity, and force of mind."

"Oh, Mrs. Debenham, how well you describe her!" said Eleanor, with tears starting into her eyes. "Yes, she is all you say."

"Mr. Newland," pursued Mrs. Debenham, pleased at the gratification she was evidently giving, "was very much concerned about the fire, and did a great deal to help the sufferers through Mr. Burrowes, without letting his name be breathed. He was much affected at the filial piety of Toby, leaping from the window with his father on his back; and since Toby got well, Mr. Newland has had him to his house, under pledge of strict secresy,

and heard all about Miss Clairvaux's kindness
to him. He would have taken him off the
stage, I believe, if Toby had not been so
averse from it himself. You see, the poor
fellow, who really is the best of the Dicks
after all, is fit for nothing but the line he has
chosen for himself; and so he prefers going
on as the manager's check-taker, to being set
up in any quiet way of business. Mr. Newland
was very much touched, I understand, by what
he said, in his curious way, of Miss Clairvaux,
and of you."

"Of me?" said Eleanor. "I don't know
what he could have said of me."

"I don't know what he said," replied Mrs.
Debenham, "but I'm sure he said something.
What Mr. Newland said of you," she added,
smiling, "was, 'that you were a pretty little
piece of French china, but that Miss Clairvaux
was real delft.'"

CHAPTER IX.

Her father loved me—oft invited me.

"AH, how delightfully cool and pretty!" exclaimed Eleanor, as Mrs. Debenham led her into the little blue room.

"This room faces the north," said Mrs. Debenham; "so it is very cold in winter, but very pleasant in summer. This door opens into my own room, my dear; so I shall be close at hand in case you want anything."

"Oh, thank you, ma'am! I am sure I

shall not want anything; but I am glad to be so near you."

" And I am glad to have you near me," said Mrs. Debenham, " for I am fond of young people. You said just now, that you had unexpectedly met an old friend. Is she staying here?"

" I spoke of a gentleman, ma'am," said Eleanor, with a warm, quick blush. " I believe he is at the Crown."

" Oh ! an old friend of your family ?"

" An old friend, and yet a young one. He was a pupil of my father's."

" And your father was a lawyer. I suppose—"

" No, ma'am, an artist. Dear me," thought Eleanor, " how inquisitive the Meadowleigh people are. They never mind what questions they ask."

" What is his name, my dear ? Is he going to stay long ?"

" His name is Day—Maurice Day," said

Eleanor. " He is of good connexions. My father was very fond of him. I don't think he is going to stay long. He only ran down just to see me, supposing me at the Peaked House, and being on short leave of absence from Rome, where the Royal Academy pay his expenses for three years, because he got the large gold medal."

" Then," said Mrs. Debenham, reviewing all these particulars in her mind, without seeming to notice Eleanor's deepening colour, " since he is disappointed of seeing you at the Peaked House, might I not as well ask him to drink tea here? Will he think it very odd?"

" Oh, ma'am, you are only too good! He would think it very kind indeed."

" Is he a very ceremonious person ?"

"Oh no! he is .... I am sure you'll like him! as you say you are fond of young people," added Eleanor more calmly, " only you must not expect too much of him."

"Then, my dear, I'll send a message to the Crown at once—or a note? Will a message do?"

"Quite, ma'am, I think."

"Because, you see, I'm not fond of writing—my joints are so stiffened with rheumatism. Perhaps, though, you would write in my name?"

"No, I would rather not, please," said Eleanor hastily; adding, as she met Mrs. Debenham's inquiring eyes, "I promised I would not—that is, I promised my mother, and he promised my father."

"Ah, I see how it is," said Mrs. Debenham, taking her hand with motherly kindness, "you promised you would not correspond with one another, till —"

"Till he had been at Rome three years; and more than a year remains," said Eleanor. "Please don't tell Mr. Debenham about it—or indeed any one."

"Well, if you particularly wish it, of course I will not."

"Indeed I particularly wish it—I tried to persuade him to go away at once, but he would stay!"

"No one can wonder much at that," naid Mrs. Debenham, laughing. "Well, I'll send my compliments to Mr. Day at the Crown, and we shall be happy to see him to tea at eight o'clock."

Instead of which, she changed her mind, going down stairs, and, without saying anything about it to Eleanor, invited him to dinner at five.

Mr. Debenham came in, a little before that time, spruce and well dressed, and greeted Eleanor very cordially.

"Well," said he, "I am glad to see all the worry and fatigue of this business has not cast you down. Burrowes has been to Stonewall. I've just seen him, and he has told me of what your mother has undertaken. She's as spirited as you are! How capitally you have made out where Miss Clairvaux is!

we were at a dead lock. Everything will go on now in due course, Mr. Newland says ; that is, if Mrs. Graydon can make out anything to the purpose ; but much depends on that. Meanwhile, we are getting together plenty of corroborative evidence—it will make a beautiful case if it comes into court. Where's Foljambe? 'Out of town?' That may be true or not."

"Sam," said his mother, " I'm expecting a visitor."

"Who can it be, mamma? Not Miss Jones, I hope."

"No, I thought of Miss Jones, with a view of entertaining Miss Graydon a little ; but this other occurred instead."

What an escape I have had, thought Eleanor.

" So you thought I could not entertain Miss Graydon," said Mr. Debenham. " Well, I think I'm as entertaining as Miss Jones, without being too vain."

"I think so too," said Eleanor laughing.

"But, dear me, who can this visitor be?"

"Somebody staying at the Crown."

"By the by, I saw a young man run up the Crown steps to-day, a most extraordinary figure —"

"Take care what you're about, Sam!" cried his mother. "He may be my visitor."

"I fancy not, mamma! Why, he had on violet stockings, and brown knickerbockers, and a blue shirt and ribbon, and a Salvator Rosa kind of hat! A handsome young dog, too, as ever I set eyes on. One of your travelling —"

Mrs. Debenham gave Eleanor a furtive look of interrogation, to which she replied by a little nod and smile, though feeling very embarrassed.

"Here he is," said Mrs. Debenham, as the visitors' bell rang.

"Not to dinner?" said Eleanor, quickly.

"Oh yes," said Mrs. Debenham, enjoying her dismay, " I improved on my invitation, going down stairs."

"Talk of a person, and he appears," ejaculated Mr. Debenham, as Maurice entered, not in his fancy walking-dress, but in ordinary dinner costume. " Who in the world can he be?" he mentally added.

. His mother advanced towards the young man with reassuring politeness, saying, as she held out her hand :

" Allow me do introduce myself to you, sir, as Mrs. Debenham. And this is my son, Mr. Debenham. Sam, this is Mr. Day, an old friend of Miss Graydon's family, a pupil of her father, just come from Rome. She met him in the town this morning, and found he had run down to see her, supposing her at the Peaked House; so, you know, I thought the pleasantest thing for all parties would be to ask Mr. Day here."

" Much the best," said Mr. Debenham,

cordially. " I'm glad to see you, Mr. Day."
Maurice had meanwhile shaken hands and
exchanged a look with Eleanor, who had
never appeared prettier.

" So you're from Rome," pursued Mr.
Debenham. " How goes on the Pope ?"

"Ah, poor old fellow! He's going off, I
think, as fast as he can."

" Seems very tenacious, though, of his
temporalities. Means to hold them, I suppose, to the last."

" The last can't be very far off, though, I
think," said Maurice. " I heard him intone,
the other day, but he gets very shaky."

" That Cardinal Whatdoyoucallhim is quite
his right hand, isn't he ?"

" Cardinal Antonelli? Oh yes, so they
say."

" He's a fine figure of a man, I suppose."

" Handsome fellow ! Such a brow ! Only
wish he'd sit to me. I'd pay him for it if he
liked."

"Oh, what, you paint? Ah, I see. An artist, studying at Rome. Exactly."

"Mr. Day got the great gold medal, Sam," put in Mrs. Debenham.

"Oh, indeed! The great—" (Dinner was here. announced). "Mr. Day, will you take down my mother? Miss Graydon, will you allow me?"

What a chatty little *partie-quarrée* it was! though the gentlemen did most of the talking: the ladies filling up the chinks; as is right.

"Well now," said Mr. Debenham, as he helped the fish, "do tell me what is the most curious thing you have seen in Rome?"

"The most curious thing I remember, at this moment to have seen there, is a black marble image of Jupiter, in St. Peter's, with Christian people bowing down before it, and kissing its toe."

"Kissing Jupiter's toe!" repeated Mrs. Debenham in dismay; "are you really speaking seriously?"

"Yes, quite seriously. I saw two old ladies in black, without bonnets, plump down on their knees last week—the last time I was at St. Peter's—and kiss the image's toe. They *call* it St. Peter, but it's known to be a statue of Jupiter."

"Dreadful," said Mrs. Debenham. "Oh, what poor, benighted people!"

"Is brigandage being put down at all?" said Mr. Debenham.

"I spent a few weeks lately in the mountains east of Rome—regular nests of brigands. I saw the lair, yet warm, of some of them; bones, and crusts, and empty bottles lying round the ashes of their fire."

"Human bones?"

"No, mutton."

"Dear me," said Mrs. Debenham, "you were very venturesome."

"That was the charm of it. The fellows, by the bye, had captured a landed proprietor, and carried him off in broad daylight from his country-house; tied him to a tree; cut off his ears bit by bit, which they remitted in instalments to his family, to extort money. Finally, skinned his nose. The ransom was then paid, and he was let off. I saw the tree to which he had been tied."

"I call that *too* venturesome," said Mrs. Debenham.

"Oh, it was the charm of it."

"My dear," said Mrs. Debenham to Eleanor, when they had left the gentlemen, "this Mr. Day of yours is a delightful companion—it is quite instructive to hear him. I hope he will not hurry away."

"I am so glad you like him!" said Eleanor. "But he ought to return to Rome."

When Maurice re-entered the drawing-room, he noticed the piano, and asked Mrs. Debenham if she played; adding, that he was very fond of music.

"I have left off playing these forty years," said she. "Perhaps you play yourself?"

"I thrum a little," he replied. "Perhaps Miss Graydon will favour us?"

But she drew back, and said, "Oh no," very decidedly.

"Come, sir," said Mrs. Debenham, "let us hear you perform, since Miss Graydon won't oblige us."

He ran his fingers through his hair, looked up at the ceiling, walked over the music-stool, and instantly began "Il Pescator;" after which he gave,

Gia del sole il splendore

in fine style; Mr. Debenham walking noise-lessly up and down the room with his hands behind him, in great satisfaction; and Mrs. Debenham beating time, and giving Eleanor looks of approval and admiration.

"I'm boring you, I know," said he, starting up, and walking to the window. "Why, actually, people are standing before the house, wondering at the row I've been making!" and he moved away.

"You really have drawn listeners," said Mr. Debenham, laughing. "Give them a little more."

"No, thank you! I won't make my singing too cheap."

At this instant, old Dr. Hurst, the rector, was announced, much to the gratification of Mrs. Debenham, who held him in great respect, though her son was accustomed to pronounce him slow.

"This is a pleasure, indeed, Dr. Hurst!" said she.

"I thought J might venture to look in," said he, "as I heard Miss Graydon was here." And though he had scarcely ever spoken to her before, he now sat down by her, and said kind things that made Eleanor's heart swell.

"I thought I should like to tell you," said he, "how we all appreciate the exertions you are making for our poor Miss Clairvaux."

"You quite surprise me, sir," said Eleanor,

"for I had thought the general feeling had been against her."

"Oh no, oh no! how should it be? when she has been so forward in every good work? How should there be a feeling against her? I go among the poor, and I know what they think and say. They say that even where she could not give money, she gave always her sympathy, sometimes her tears. Against her? O no, O no! quite the reverse."

And then a long talk about her ensued, in which Mr. Debenham was diplomatic. It turned out, however, that everybody knew as much as everybody else; Maurice through Eleanor, and Doctor Hurst through Mr. Burrowes. So when they found this out, they all spoke freely. And sometimes there were refreshing pauses, when people enjoyed the evening air stealing through the open windows.

Mrs. Debenham was pleased that Doctor Hurst should see her handsome tea-service, and taste her rich seed cake.

"As I came along," said he, "I heard a fine, rich voice in the distance, and saw people standing in the street. Could the singing be here?"

"The singer sits opposite to you," said Mr. Debenham. "He ought to sing well, for he comes from Italy. Strait from Rome, sir! saw the Pope perform mass last week!"

"Ah, I should like to see Rome," said Doctor Hurst. "Who would not? A place so teeming with associations, Pagan and Christian! Pray, sir, were you ever down in the Catacombs?"

"Yes, sir. I have lost myself in them."

"Oh dear, oh dear!" said the doctor.

"Maurice, that was very bad of you," said Eleanor hastily, on which Mr. Debenham gave her a quick look.

"Of course I did not do so on purpose. Nobody would. I was copying inscriptions."

"Some of them are very touching, I believe?" said Doctor Hurst.

"Very, sir. I have one or two in my pocket-book, that I copied."

He produced them and handed them to him.

"Dear me, these are very curious, and very beautiful."

"Will you oblige me by accepting them, sir? I have them by heart."

"Certainly I should like to accept them very much indeed, if you really can spare them. Thank you! thank you very much. Dear, dear, how many interesting things you must have seen at Rome. The Mamertine prison? the Vatican Library? the fawn of Praxiteles?"

"I have seen them all, sir,"

Before the evening had closed, they all felt on the footing of old, established friends. Maurice sang again, at Dr. Hurst's request; and, on his asking for sacred music, Eleanor sang "What though I trace each herb and flower," and played Mozart's "Et resurrexit:" fourth mass, in C.

When Maurice wished good night, Mrs. Debenham said, "What are you going to do to-morrow, sir?"

"Sketch Stonewall, ma'am."

"Nonsense," said Eleanor, laughing.

"Positively I am."

"No, no," said Mr. Debenham, "there really is nothing to sketch there. If you go to Lurdane Grange, you may find some pretty pickings."

And as he accompanied him to the door, he directed him how to reach it.

"I've engaged him to dine here afterwards," said he, coming back. "Well, Miss Graydon, I like Mr. Day extremely. I give my consent! Oh, he told me all about everything!"

"Ah, he is a wretched hand at keeping anything to himself;" said Eleanor. "I only wish he would content himself with telling his own secrets. At any rate, I hope *you* will respect them."

"Oh, of course," said he smiling, as he

shook hands with her, and wished her good night. "Only secrets leak out somehow in Meadowleigh, one never knows how. There's that Burrowes, always going from house to house, is trusted by everybody, hears everything, tells everything, and yet nobody is angry with him. Besides, he finds out things at a glance. Directly he sees you and Day together, he'll know all about it."

"Ah," said Eleanor, wincing a little, "he saw us to-day."

When she was shut into her little blue room at last, she screened the light of her wax candle, and stood looking behind the window-blind into the dark. The moon was drifting fast through troubled clouds. Was her mother watching it? Was Miss Clairvaux? Poor Miss Clairvaux!

CHAPTER X.

To try wrong guesses is, with most persons, the only way to hit upon right ones.—WHEWELL.

DURING the next three days, Maurice managed to make himself talked about by the whole town; and his appearance was so prepossessing that everybody's word was a good one. Those eyes of his—that smile —that irresistible costume—were too much for the malleable hearts in Meadowleigh— if he had not been such a good young man, he'd have been too captivating by half.

Secure of his having gone off with sketch-book and camp-stool to Lurdane Grange, Eleanor made several visits of enquiry among Miss Clairvaux's poorer neighbours, openly mentioning her object, and talking over with them various little circumstances which they brought to light. Sometimes she was able to explain away things that had puzzled them; at other times, they mentioned little traits that secretly puzzled her. Could poor Miss Clairvaux be a little, a very little . . . no, she thought not.

Her last visit was to Claudia, who blushed like a rose, at being caught talking at the gate with a good-looking young man; one of the Fords. Eleanor was close upon them before they saw her. Ford shouldered his mattock and swung down the lane at his first glimpse of her, and Claudia was ready to run in-doors, but changed her mind and held the gate open. Eleanor had too much fellow-feeling for her to make her uncomfortable.

"Well, Claudia, here I am again, you see," she said.

"Oh, miss, it's quite a comfort to see you. I feel so disconsolate sometimes."

They had a talk in-doors, and then Eleanor left her. Who should be awaiting her, outside, but Maurice!

"I thought you were miles away!" said she. "How *could* you find me out?"

"I suppose I've a tongue in my head. And eyes too. Never trust to my not finding you out!"

"You did not go, then, to Lurdane Grange! Where have you been?"

"To Stonewall."

"Now, Maurice!"

"I have. I had determined I would. Nothing ever shakes my purpose."

"What did you do there?"

"Sat down on my camp-stool and sketched the wall. An old woman presently looked out of an upper window. See, here she is.

She coughed, I coughed. She continued looking at me. I presented a small pocket-telescope. She ducked. Presently she appeared again, attended by a man. The man ducked. Presently he opened the gate and came out. This was precisely what I had wanted. 'Are you employed by authority?' 'I am not.' 'Oh!' and with a snort he retired. I continued to draw. Presently he returned. 'Master says, if you are not employed by authority, you had better go away.' 'My compliments to your master, and I shall have respectful pleasure in complying with his advice.'

"But come," said he, in an altered tone, I want you to show me the Peaked House."

They walked thither, sat down on the undulating turf a little way above it, and remained there some time; talking seriously and sadly. The clarionet of a wandering musician sounded plaintively in the distance. The air was 'Home, sweet home!' Miss

Clairvaux's home looked melancholy and neglected; a white hen and chickens were pecking among the flower-beds unmolested.

"I should like to see this poor Miss Clairvaux before I return," said Maurice, "but I suppose I shall not. There's the old woman taking a reconnoissance! She can't make us out."

"She can't make *you* out," said Eleanor, "for she knows me. Perhaps she takes you for one of the circus people," with a mischievous glance at his dress. Maurice considered any tribute to it a compliment, therefore did not at all resent it.

"Here comes the little dog," said he, as Fly came running from the house to spring into Eleanor's lap, and look wistfully at her with its large dark eyes.

"Poor little fellow!" said she, caressing him, "you look half starved, and very wretched. Poor Fly!"

The old woman here came to the gate,

calling, "Dash! Dash!" and finding the spaniel did not attend to her, she toiled up the slope to Eleanor.

"I wish, miss," said she, civilly, "you'd be good enough to tell me the dog's name, for he won't answer to any I can think of, and I'm afraid of letting him out, because I can't call him back; so he gets no exercise at all, poor thing."

"Nor food either, does he?" said Maurice, whom she had been furtively eyeing all the while. "My good lady, air and exercise will increase his appetite—it increases mine. Don't you find it so with yourself?"

"Ah, sir," said she, very glad to have a few words to exchange with him, "I have not much to eat, any more than the dog, for Mr. Horsefield pays my board-wages very irregularly, and allows nothing for the dog, but I can't let him starve, pretty fellow— (Fly, is that is name, miss? Thank you!) I do assure you, sir, I'm pretty near as bad off

as Miss Clairvaux, for if she's kept on bread
and water, I've only bread and tea, and if
she's in solitary confinement, so am I, with
no one to pity me. I daren't leave the house,
nobody comes into it, and all the rooms are
locked up but the kitchen and attic."

"That's impressive," said Maurice. "But,
bread and water! Is Miss Clairvaux really
kept on that?"

"Indeed I don't know, sir, so pray don't
repeat it against me. I only said, *if* she were
kept on that, I hadn't much better."

"Well," said Eleanor, "it is hard you should
have to keep the dog, and I am very pleased
at your being kind to it. It is not my
property any more than yours, but I love
dumb animals, so, if you please, I will pay
sixpence a week towards his keep, for the
present at any rate, and begin with a month's
pay in advance."

"Thank you kindly, miss," said the old
woman, as she took the florin. "Fly shall

have milk and meat too, out of this. I'm sure it's no pleasure to me to be here, and very little profit. The very tradesmen's lads that call, look on me as if I was a witch!"

"Ah, they'll be glad to have Miss Clair-vaux back, no doubt," said Maurice. "In the first place, they like her, and in the second, she's a better customer."

"You might put that first, sir, generally."

"Do you know where Miss Clairvaux is?" said Eleanor.

"No, miss, I know nothing about the business in any way, except that Mr. Fol-jambe put me here, and bade me keep the previous occupants out."

She looked regretfully after them, as they walked away.

"So there is a crook in every lot," said Eleanor. "Even this old woman is to be pitied."

"And Fly," said Maurice. "Can't say I pity the old woman much. Nor am I conscious, at this moment, of any crook in *my* lot."

"What a cordial, pleasant expression 'thank you kindly' is!" said Eleanor. "I always feel that it overpays me for any little obligation."

"Then, when I have the luck to get married," said Maurice, "as I hope I shall before I am many months older, I'll say when I put the ring on my bride's finger—'Thank you kindly!'—Eleanor, how should you like to live in Italy?"

"Oh, I could not bear to live away from mamma!"

"But if she were to come, too —"

"She could not leave George."

"Is George going to be in leading-strings all his life?"

"No, but he must have a home."

"The sooner he makes one for himself, then, the better."

"The inclination is not wanting, but he

must wait. Surely, *you* do not want to make Rome your permanent home?"

"One gets very good commissions there, sometimes, from travellers. And then, it is a great thing to have such sublime works of art always before one. An old, red rag, hanging out of an upper window—a broken jug with a flower planted in it, have a positive beauty in that atmosphere which unites distinctness with such exquisite softness. Somebody has well said that light literally *paints* in Italy."

"Still, 'home, sweet home' has more attractions for me than an old red rag, however brilliant."

"Yes, *cara*, but think of a moonlight visit to the Colosseum, or a noonday stroll in the gardens of Villa Borghese!"

"Ah, I should like that, because it would remind me of Miriam and Donatello! But, Maurice, I don't think it can be so easy to plod on with one's every day duties in a land where everything allures to luxury and amusement."

"Everything? *I* plod on, pretty hard there, I can tell you —"

"But the very climate must tempt to slothful ease —"

"What of that, if one does not yield to the temptation? There are not many *agrémens*, I assure you, in my lodging in a dirty little lane out of the Via della Ripetta. Not over-fresh, not over-clean."

"Why do you live there, then?"

"It is cheap. And it is but like the nest of a bird that is on the wing all day, and forgets itself in sleep all night. Till Sophy came, I got my meals at a café where all the artists go: and now I often dine, like Salvator Rosa, on a handful of fresh figs."

"Have you heard from Sophy lately?"

"No."

"Perhaps you have not written to her."

"Oh, Sophy and I don't have much to say to one another now."

"I shall be very sorry if I have been the cause of any coolness—"

"Nothing of the kind. Oh no, we are just on the same terms we always were."

"I am glad to hear that; only, before she went to Italy, you used to write her such delightful long letters."

"Perhaps a little bird told me that some one else would hear them read," said Maurice slyly.

"Oh, I *hope* you had some better motive than that!"

"How could I have a better?"

"Easily—because that would be a very bad one."

"I am afraid I had a very bad one."

"I think you like to make yourself out worse than you are."

"It is generally the other way. Men

mostly try to make themselves out better than they are. Do you prefer that plan?"

"Well, it argues more humility. But I would sooner that people tried to appear neither worse nor better than they were, but in their proper colours."

"I revealed myself in my proper colours when I confessed to taking some pains with my letters to Sophy, for the sake of somebody else."

"Ah, well, I'm sorry to hear it."

"Honestly? *Non lo credo, nò !*"

"You *may* believe it."

"I would not if I could, and I could not if I would."

"Maurice! I am afraid your organ of self-esteem is very largely developed."

"What, because I said I could not, and would not believe that you were really sorry I had taken additional pains with my letters to Sophy, because I thought she would lend them, or read them to you? I could as soon believe in the Pope. Poor old fellow, I wish he were safely pensioned off somewhere—in Brighton or Hastings for instance."

"There are plenty of foreign watering-places for him."

"But he would do you no harm—you need not be afraid of him. One drop of prussic acid won't poison a whole tank of fresh water. As I came by the Quirinal the other day, I saw the Pope's washing hanging out to dry, from eleven windows. If the same thing were done at Buckingham Palace, we should hardly think it good taste."

"What can you expect of an old bachelor?"

This epithet, as applied by Eleanor, had something in it which so tickled Maurice's fancy, that he laughed immoderately. I rather think he was in that happy mood in which one is ready to laugh at anything or nothing. And though Eleanor was anxious and saddened whenever she thought of her absent friend, it was impossible to resist the genial influence of the friend near at hand.

All this time, it may be observed, anything like direct love-making was tolerably avoided; and yet it was certain that they understood each other as well as if they had talked of nothing else. Instead of being like persons on the confines of an engagement they were bound not to make, they rather were like a couple long engaged; so long, that all the preliminary stages of courtship had given place to the sober certainty of waking bliss. How far were these young persons, then, justifiable in having arrived at this point of good understanding? Why, in the first place, they had made some progress towards it in earlier days, even before Eleanor's father had begun to suppose that an attachment might spring up between them, and certainly long before he thought it had done so. What vows of boyish fidelity had then been uttered, must remain unknown; but it must be borne in mind, that Mrs. Graydon had not told Miss Clairvaux such vows had never been made; she had only declared that they had not been made to her knowledge; but she had distinctly said that Maurice had *looked* love, even if he did not name it; and that if his words said nothing, his manner said everything. It was all very well for Mr. Graydon to say, " I insist on your not naming love to Eleanor—" there is no proof that Maurice ever answered " very well, sir, I will not." On the contrary, there is every reason to think he would be sure to say nothing of the sort.

On the other hand, there is no reason to think Mr. Graydon had ever been so unwise as to say to his daughter, " You are not to think of Maurice ;" which might naturally have brought him involuntarily into her head. No, he warned the young man in a general way, and he left Eleanor unalarmed. She knew nothing of the interview between them

before Maurice went to Rome; when he had
begged so hard to go away engaged, and Mr.
Graydon had refused. Maurice had pledged
himself to him, but not to her, to consider
himself engaged. And yet, when he took
leave of her in her parents' presence, and had
clasped her hand for a minute, while he
said, "I shall come back again in three
years—" the look that accompanied those
simple words, had told her unmistakeably,
that he would then come back *for her;* and
though he could not be sued for that look in
a court of law, should he change his mind,
she believed in him, and now she felt that her
belief was not unfounded.

Still, though as her mother expressed it,
she took it very nicely, she had drooped a
little after he went away; and Mrs. Graydon
had spoken upon it, and said: "Eleanor, it
is plain to see that Maurice is very sorry to
leave you," &c., which made the young girl
feel she was sympathized with, and yet

o 2

supplied her with a motive for not giving way.
She knew it to be true that they were then
quite too young and quite unprovided, and
had a pretty correct idea that if Maurice had
asked her of her father, a decided *no* would
have been his answer. Being a very sweet-
tempered girl, she had, therefore, uncom-
plainingly adopted for her motto the good old
axiom "Duties are ours, events are God's."

But then, when her father died, and
Maurice wrote so passionately to her from
Rome, she knew beyond a doubt how she
was loved, and would gladly have plighted
herself to him in return. But Mrs. Graydon
then told her that if she did so, she would act
counter to the wish of her father, who had
been aware of Maurice's attachment, and had
approved it, but had not wished any positive
engagement to take place, or correspondence
to be carried on, till the three years were out;
"and they are half over already," said Mrs.
Graydon, "and the other half will soon be

gone, and you can send him a kind message through Sophy, and that will be just the same."

Eleanor did not feel it *would* be just the same, by any means; but her father's wishes had now double force, and therefore she adopted the very inadequate alternative that her mother suggested. Perhaps this was no bad thing for Maurice, whose sanguine, happy temper had made him almost as much a favourite of fortune as that lady who "never had a cross, except a diamond one." Here was a hope to work and wait for; and he found work the best remedy for the tedium of waiting. Besides, he loved his art, almost as much as he loved Eleanor: loved it for its own sake, as well as for the hope of its leading him to fame. And—it may be a mistake—but I do suppose that a thorough artist, very much in love, and almost driven to distraction, might find himself involuntarily recalled to his senses by a bell-shaped fold in a curtain, or a sudden gleam of sunlight on a distant hill-top, too fleeting and precious not to be booked on the instant.

Well, whatever he might have gone through in the interim, here was Maurice at hand again, looking by no means the victim of a blighted attachment, but healthy and merry, and as if he had no particular load on his conscience. Was Eleanor, therefore, to say, " go back to Rome" more than once? She had said so once or twice, if not very peremptorily; and, if he would not go, who was to make him? Besides, it seemed so natural and allowable to take up their pleasant intercourse just when it had been broken off, that she may have been led into weak compliance, and if it were so, I can only express regret.

As they returned to the town, they passed Miss Thompson's school, taking their morning walk, two and two. The girls looked demurely down as they passed, yet every one of them had noticed Maurice, and thought how fortunate was Miss Graydon to have such a companion. Miss Jones watched them over her wire-gauze blind.

"The reconciliation, then, has been effected," thought she. "Ah well, I'm glad of it, I can't bear young hearts to be sad. I wonder what lovers' nonsense they quarrelled about."

Some days had now elapsed, and Eleanor became uneasy at her mother's silence. Maurice, meanwhile, had run up to town, to report himself to the Academy. Somehow he contrived to make his story good. During this pause, no intercourse took place between Eleanor and Mr. Newland. He had relapsed into his valetudinarian habits and resumed his beloved literary employments. One morning, however, the post brought Eleanor a short note from him, and a very thick packet from her mother. The short note ran thus :

"Stonewall House, July 23rd.

" My dear young Lady,

" Has Mrs. Graydon reported any progress yet? This long silence surprises me. Pray let me hear any news you may have received from her, good or bad.

"Your faithful servant,
" VALENTINE NEWLAND."

Putting this missive unconcernedly aside, Eleanor eagerly opened her mother's packet and devoured its contents, which were as follows :

Starveling Hold, July 20th.

" My dear love, how could you think of sending your old mother off to Cheshire instead of Staffordshire? There are no Clairvauxes in this county! I do not regret, however, having come here in the first instance ; having had such a desire to see the place once more ; but how different things appear to

young eyes and old ones ! At fourteen, I was
quite in love with the romance of the spot;
at forty-three, it seems to me the most forlorn
place imaginable !

" You know, Starveling Hold is only the
nickname given it because it was the residence
of an old miser, who starved himself to death;
however, it has been used so long that it is
now considered the regular name. I used to
delight in the gloom of the old, dusty rooms,
with carpetless floors, tattered hangings, and
empty fire-places, only lighted through the
round holes in the closed shutters. I remember amusing myself by weaving a long
romance about a beautiful girl succeeding to
the property, and coming to take possession,
and routing out hoards of guineas and bank-
notes behind the wainscots, and under the
hearthstones, and inside bolsters and mat-
tresses; becoming quite a Miss Burdett
Coutts with her wealth, relieving widows and
orphans, founding schools and churches, &c.

I could not weave such a romance now, if you offered me a thousand pounds for it!

"Well; I slept at A—, came on the next morning to B—, left the railway, inquired my way, found it involved a walk of some miles, and started off. I enjoyed it exceedingly for a mile or two; but the heat then became so great, that I was glad to sit down under a hedge and eat a roll I had brought with me. I drank, out of my hand, from a clear little stream close by. It seemed very pleasant! An old shepherd, with a crook, and a dog at his heels, presently left watching his flock to stare at me. I had a little talk with him— asked if any family of the name of Clairvaux had ever lived in the neighbourhood. No,— there had been a family once, of the name of—Chubb! maybe I meant them!

" He directed me to a short cut across a moor, and I started off again. It was very pleasant; but rather too lonely. The wild animals put me in mind of Alexander Selkirk's words (as applied by Cowper—)

> "They are so unaccustomed to man,
> Their tameness is shocking to me!

"I don't know why it should have been so, but all the scraps of poetry I had learnt when a girl, came into my head; and especially a line which I don't know to this moment, whether I remembered or invented—

> "Sweet Nature's lovely face can never tire!

"It is very true, at any rate.

"Well, at length I found myself on a shadeless by-road, with a cart coming along it; and, do you know, I was so hot and tired, that I bargained with the man, a good-natured, clownish fellow, to give me a lift. It was a sort of dray, that went very slowly, and shook me a good deal; still it gave me a rest. I found it impossible to get up any conversation with the driver. However, finding where I was going, he took me almost all the way; and then set me down at the corner of a cross-road, saying, 'you must go down there, mistress.' I gave him sixpence, and proceeded down the road. The next turn brought me in sight of Starveling Hold—I knew it at once, though after the lapse of so many years. I thought it looked less ruinous and miserly than formerly. Arrived at the wide old porch, with stone seats in it, I raised the latch. 'Come in,' said some one inside. I went in; and there, all alone in that old kitchen, sat he whom we used to call 'Uncle Joel,' though he was no uncle of mine. 'Who are you?' said he, removing his pipe from his mouth, and looking askance at me. 'I'm Ellen Barker, that was,' said I, 'don't you remember me, Uncle Joel?' 'You Ellen Barker?' said he slowly. 'Why, you're no more like her than I'm like you!' However, I convinced him I was myself; so then he was very friendly, and so was Aunt Madge, as I used to call her (though no relation), when she came in. They made me eat and drink of their best, and pressed me to stay. So I accepted a bed for one night at least, and here I am, writing in my room, at a little past nine, that being the family hour for going to bed. I think it must have been the room the old miser died in; at any rate, it is very eerie. From the low, raftered ceiling hang bags of seeds, corn-samples, and other things that they want to keep out of reach of the rats. Under the bed are hampers of keeping-apples, which, I should say by their smell, have been kept too long. There is also, a strong smell of cheese; so that altogether, the room, though large and rambling, is anything but fresh, and I hear rats and mice behind the wainscot, and animals of a larger growth, stamping in a stable underneath.

"Tired as I am, I cannot sleep till I have written to you, though I have nothing important to say. During the evening, we had a long talk, chiefly about my affairs, for they

don't seem to have any of their own, except
when to brew, and when to bake, and how
many cheeses to make, and how much butter.
I asked Uncle Joel if he knew of any Clairvauxes in these parts. He repeated the name
several times, ' Clairvaux ? Clairvaux ? No, I
can't say I do. No, I never heard it before.' Aunt Madge said the same, and so
said an old farmer who dropped in. I had
not depended much on them, and you know
I wished to see them for personal reasons;
so that I was not altogether disappointed.
Still, I was sorry not to make any progress
whatever in the matter in hand. Perhaps I
may not. It is all in the hands of Providence.
And now, good night, my dear child. Perhaps in the morning, when I am rested, I
may see my way clearer than I do just
now.

"Thursday. After writing the above, I
went to bed; and though the mattress
seemed stuffed with unboiled potatoes, I slept

soundly till daybreak, when I was aroused by all sorts of farm-house noises. When I went down, I found Aunt Madge busy in her dairy, the servant-maid assisting her, and Uncle Joel smoking—just as I had left him overnight.

"'Oh, I didn't expect to see you down yet,' said he. 'We're early folk, and obliged to be so; but I thought you town-madams lay a-bed till noon.'

"I assured him I always rose early. "Don't you think,' said he, after a little pause, 'that the name of the people you were inquiring after over-night, might be Clearvoice? I never heard of any Clare-voes in this country; but there was a lot of Clearvoices used to be at a Staffordshire place, called Hackery Corner, though I don't know that any of them are left now. I've spelt their names on the tombstones many a time.' 'Do you remember how you spelt it?' said I. "C, l, a, i, r, (Clear) v, a, u, x,

(voice),' said he. So here was the very name
I wanted! 'How can I get to the place?'
said I. 'l'm going to send over a calf there,
by-and-by,' said he. 'I suppose you wouldn't
like to go in the same cart?' Well, it was
not very pleasant; but I had pre-determined
not to be deterred by any difficulties, and
on inquiry, I found there was no other way
whatever of getting to Hackery Corner,
except by walking, or riding a cart-horse!
The distance was beyond a walk; and, you
know, Eleanor, I am no rider, even if there
had been a lady's horse at command. So
I accepted the seat in the cart, and Uncle
Joel then told me that Hackery Corner
belonged to a farmer named Thudge, a very
worthy sort of man, and one who, on his
recommendation, would be sure to assist me
in any way he could. So I begged his good
offices with Farmer Thudge; and after a very
friendly leave-taking, (letting it remain very
uncertain whether I should come back to

them or not), I started in the cart. The poor calf cried piteously for its mother all the way; and we left the poor mother lowing after her in the stable. I felt for them both. What a pity animals must be killed!

"We went along a road that gradually ascended higher and higher, till we got to a wild sort of upland where the air was deliciously fresh. The driver said:

"'Now, missis, you be in Staffordshire— 'this be the Moorland.' We scarcely met a living soul all the way; those we did meet were uncouth and hard-featured. The fields were divided with stone walls.

"At length we reached this rambling old farm-house, and I was so stiffened with jolting that I could hardly step out of the cart. An elderly, farmer-like looking man came out, and looked pleasantly at me. 'Well now, I can't think who you do be,' said he. 'I'm a stranger, sir,' said I, 'but my name is Graydon, and I suppose yours is Thudge.'

'That's my name, and a queer one,' said he. So then I told him Uncle Joel had promised me his good offices while I remained a short time in the neighbourhood; and he at once said he and his 'good woman' would make me as comfortable as they could."

CHAPTER XI.

He whom, e'en in life's last stage,
Endeavours laudable engage,
Is paid, at least in peace of mind,
And sense of having well designed.

HERE ended fytte the first of Mrs. Graydon's letter; the second was on different paper, in different ink, and written much smaller and less legibly.

"Friday morning.

"My dear Eleanor, we had such an extraordinary conversation last night! I must begin by telling you that Mrs. Thudge is a very nice person indeed—a motherly, friendly, neighbourly woman. She and her husband call each other father and mother, and sometimes thee and thou each other. I told them of my visit to Starveling Hold, and how I stayed there when a girl, and what a pleasant place it had then seemed to me, and how they thought *me* changed in the interval. Farmer Thudge and his wife had dined at twelve, and were now preparing for their four o'clock tea ; and a most hospitable spread it was, with the strongest of tea, the richest of cream, brown bread warm from the oven, new laid eggs, fried ham, and honey in the comb. Hungry as I was, my appetite was appeased long before they ceased pressing me to eat. By the time tea was over, we were the best of friends. Mrs. Thudge then went to her dairy ; and the farmer, who was nursing a lamed foot, placed me opposite him in the porch, where the air stealing in through the honey-suckle was deliciously

sweet and fresh. 'And so you've two children,' said he. 'The son is training for a
doctor; and the daughter—?' 'My daughter,'
said I, ' has, or rather has had a most comfortable situation in the house of a Miss Clairvaux .... a curious name, by the by.' 'Not
so curious to my ears as you may think,'
said he, after smoking his pipe a little. ' I
know the name very well : the Clairvauxes
had property once in this county—my father
worked under them. However, they're all
extinct, I believe, now.'—'Were they good
sort of people?' said I. 'Very good sort of
people,' said he. 'Because,' said I, 'goodness and badness sometimes seem to run
in families, just like gout and insanity.'
' Goodness ran in the Clairvaux family,' said
he. 'And insanity too, perhaps,' said I.
' Not that I ever heard of,' said he, 'nor
gout either—and I should be likely to know,
for my father worked for them before me,
and his father before him.' This seemed a

very satisfactory approach to the point. 'Oh, *you* worked for them, did you?' said I. 'Scared away the crows,' said he, 'when I was a little boy.'

"His face, on this, became full of thought, . and even troubled; he continued smoking, while I sat in silence, thinking how favourable his testimony was, as far as it went.

"'What curious creatures we do be,' resumed he presently; 'how our little sins, or sins we think little, get bigger and bigger after they're committed, and lie like a dead weight on our hearts.' 'That's very true,' said I. 'Truer than you think, or can know,' said he. 'Why now, I remember a scrape I got into when I was a boy, that I've never spoke of to this day, even to my wife; and yet at this moment I remember all about it, as well as if it happened yesterday. You see, I was fond of fishing; and there was a bright, deep trout-stream in which we were forbidden to fish, because the squire liked keeping the trout to himself. Well, what does I, one certain evening, but go a fishing in this trout-stream; mainly because 'twas forbidden. Didn't catch anything, though; for why? 'twas getting too dark; leastways, that was one reason. I don't suppose you care to hear about it, though?' ' Yes, I care very much,' said I. ' Well,' said he, ' I don't know what possesses me to tell you, but somehow I'm impelled. Maybe, when I've done so, I shall get it off my mind. Well, as I was saying, I couldn't catch anything; so I turned about and set my face homeward; sulky-like at having caught nothing.

" 'Well, I was keeping along the river's bank, yet not too near, when I saw a man coming along the water-side. Thinks I, that's the squire's keeper, he'll guess what I've been after, and beat me within an inch of my life. 'Twas no good to dodge him. If I'd turned about and run away, he'd have been upon me

in no time, with those long legs of his, and
seized me by the scruff of my neck. At least,
I thought so at the moment. I proceeded
to slip by him, innocent-like, between him
and the bushes. But he kept so close to
them, that I was obliged to pass between
him and the river. 'Who's that?' says he.
'Is it you, Harry?—what are you about?'
Then I knew by the voice, and also by the
face, it was not the keeper, but Parson Clairvaux. I didn't care for him as much as for
the other, for he was kind to us boys, but I
turned sheepish-like, and, sheering a little
nearer the water to make room for him, my
foot slipped, and head over heels I went back-
ward plump into the river. I bobbed up
again the next minute, and saw him reaching
after me, and then heard a splash. I saw
no more, for down I went again the next
moment, and felt him catch hold of me and
drag me to land. But the next moment, he
let go of me, and I, finding my feet touch the

ground, scrambled out up the bank, and took
to my heels, and never looked behind, but
ran straight home, and went right up to bed,
without saying nothing to nobody. Now,
wasn't I a bad boy?'"

When Eleanor reached this, she laid down
the letter, for her eyes were so full of tears,
that she could not see to read. Mrs. Graydon went on—

"'You may imagine how I felt! the dis-
closure seemed providential; nay, was so, I
am assured. At this moment, Mrs. Thudge
came up to us, and said, 'what is all this
about, father?' 'About my being a very bad
boy,' said he, in a softened voice, taking her
hand. 'Ah, that I'll never believe,' said she.
'True, though,' said he, 'as true as you're
there; however, Mrs. Graydon, I didn't know,
mind you, that the parson was drowned. I
concluded he had scrambled out the same as
I did; and, in fact, I didn't think much about
him, my principal care being to get out of

his way before he recognized me. But
drowned he was, though. And found
drowned next day. Then I felt awful; but
it didn't occur to me to say anything; or
rather, I was afraid. It couldn't have brought
him back to life, you see, and I didn't consider it had been anyways my fault, only my
misfortune; but when I heard there was going
to be a crowner's inquest, my heart failed me
dreadful. I thought the laws might hang
me, and there was no chance for me but to
hold my tongue. So I held my tongue;
and the verdict brought in was, 'found
drowned.'"

"At this point," continued Mrs. Graydon;
"I could forbear no longer; but starting up,
I shook Farmer Thudge's hand violently, and
then kissed his wife; at which they both
looked surprised enough. 'Oh, you don't
know what good news this is to me!' said
I. 'Good?' repeated he, looking mystified,
'why, how should it be that, when it's about

the accidental death of as good a young
parson as ever lived ?'

"'Then I told him how much depended
on its being proved that his death *was*
accidental; and I cried a little, and Mrs.
Thudge cried too, and the farmer cried, because, he said, it was such an exposition of
the text, ' be sure your sin will find you out.'
' Here,' said he, ' have I, through my sin,
and my concealment, caused an innocent
lady to be unnecessarily put into confinement.'

" I asked him if he would have any objection to make a deposition to the effect of what
he had told me. ' No,' he said, ' not at all;
he owed it to the lady, and could not be easy
till he had done so. He would send for the
lawyer in the morning.'

" And the lawyer is now being fetched.
I do not know whether I have secured all the
evidence Mr. Newland desires for the benefit
of Miss Clairvaux; and shall therefore remain

with these kind people till I have heard from
you on that point.   We sat up talking long
beyond their usual bed-time, and I heard
many interesting things of the Clairvauxes,
which I have not space for now.   Oh, how
glad I am that God put it into my mind
to come here !   I could do nothing of myself;
but you see all difficulties have been smoothed.
Let dear George know all about it.

  " I remain, my beloved child,

   " Your ever affectionate mother,

     " ELLEN GRAYDON."

The   deposition,   properly   attested,   was
inclosed.

Eleanor spent a few minutes in fervent
thanksgiving, and supplication for grace to
carry through the good work ; and then
hastened in search of Mrs. Debenham.   She
found her and her son together in the dining-
parlour.   They knew by her excited look
that she had important news of some sort

to communicate, and were eager to hear it.

She began by attempting to read her mother's letter to them; but finding she could not command her voice, she gave it to Mr. Debenham, and begged him to read it aloud. Exclamations, congratulations, felicitations succeeded one another. "Only," said Mr. Debenham, "we must not hallo till we get out of the wood."

"I must let Mr. Newland know without delay," said Eleanor.

"It is a long way for you to go, my dear," said Mrs. Debenham. "I will send to the Crown for one of their nice open britzkas, and will drive over to Stonewall with you."

"Oh, thank you!"

"This deposition is all right, as far as it goes," said Mr. Debenham. "Well, mamma, I'm going down the town—I'll tell Fuller to send you up his best britzka, and best horse

—not the broken-kneed one, nor yet the one that jibs "

Much as Eleanor wished to acknowledge her mother's letter, she thought it best not to do so till she had seen Mr. Newland. Indeed, there would not have been time to do so, for the britzka was at the door almost immediately.

" I shall drive gently round the Green till you come out," said Mrs. Debenham.

" Oh no, ma'am; please come in !"

" It might not be agreeable to Mr. Newland."

Eventually, it was agreed that they should send in their cards together, and leave Mr. Newland to decide for himself.

The decision was against Mrs. Debenham. Mr. Newland presented his compliments—he was so very poorly this morning, as to be quite unequal to seeing Mrs. Debenham. He would make an effort to see Miss Graydon.

The effort apparently wanting, was to make himself a little smarter—for he did not seem more poorly than usual; though there was a plaintive tone at first in his voice, that was a little got up.

"Well, my dear young lady," said he, in this Peter Grievous way. Then suddenly changing his note, and starting to his feet, "But what! but what! Roses in cheeks, and diamonds in eyes? There's good news in the wind, or I'm not a sinner!"

"There is good news, sir, I think," said Eleanor, "though I am afraid of laying too much stress on it. Mamma says—But perhaps you will like to read her letter."

"Very much, very much;—that is, if she does not cross," taking up his double eye-glass as he spoke. Eleanor gave him the first half, reserving the sequel, and also the deposition.

"Good hand, good hand. Hum, hum, hum—very tender and affectionate. A long while since I've read a lady's letter—I had almost forgotten how well ladies could write :

hum, hum—graphic—graphic." And he ran through fytte the first, and handed it back to her with a disappointed air. " Graphic, graphic, graphic; but not a bit to the point. ' Words, words, words,' as Hamlet says."

" Will you please to finish it, sir ?" said Eleanor humbly, as she offered him fytte the second. He set to work upon it with less avidity; but directly he came to the words " extraordinary conversation," his eyes kindled like coals. Not an exclamation, not an expletive did he utter, but the silent workings of his face were something remarkable. In the midst, Mr. Burrowes came suddenly in, with his cheerful,

" My dear sir—!" but was thrown all on a heap by Mr. Newland's loud

" Not a word, on your life !" his hand being flung out towards him at the same time, to enforce silence. Mr. Burrowes dropped into the nearest chair, exchanging a look with

Eleanor, who observed Mr. Debenham on tip-
toe in the background.

Suddenly Mr. Newland shouted, " Huzza,
huzza! Why have I not a wig or night-cap to
throw up? Here's the finest testimony con-
ceivable, we must get a regular deposition. '

" Here it is, sir."

" You don't say so! Wonderful, wonderful!
I must calm myself. I'm all in a tremble. I
can't read a word. My ears ring with hollow
murmurs."

" Take a glass of wine, sir—" said Mr.
Burrowes.

" You're right, Burrowes! oblige me by
ringing the bell. Ring it smartly. John,
you rascal! bring us a bottle of wine. Do
you hear, sir? a bottle of Tokay."

Then, passing his hand over his eyes—

"My sight is a little confused to-day.
Bilious, I suppose, Burrowes? I wish Mr.
Debenham were here."

"Here I am, sir," said Mr. Debenham, stepping forward.

"You here? Ha, ha, ha, why, it's like a scene in a play!"

His laugh had, to Eleanor's heart, something pathetic in it.

The wine was brought in, and handed round. He insisted on Eleanor's tasting it; and drank his own with eagerness.

"Now, I'm my own man again," said he, sighing, as he passed his hand over his eyes, "the motes have disappeared. What, what! I must not give way, when so much lies before me. I'm going to make an effort. I am going to London."

"Sir, Sir!" expostulated Mr. Burrowes.

"I *am*, Burrowes!"

"Then let me go with you!"

"I will *not!*"

This was said in a tone that silenced remonstrance.

"Oblige me, Mr. Debenham," said he in

a softer tone, "by running through that deposition, and seeing if it's all right."

"It is, sir. I have gone through it already."

"That's well. Do either of you happen to have a hundred pounds about you?"

"No, sir!" said they simultaneously.

"I'll write a cheque, then, and send John to get it cashed; only, generally, I do not charge him with so much." He pulled the bell with energy.

"John, you dog, put on your best livery. Make yourself fine, sirrah, make yourself fine! John, I'm going to London!"

John looked ready to faint away.

"And I'm going to take you with me, John—" John revived.

"So, (take a glass of wine, my poor fellow). "So, clean the post-chariot, John, air the cushions well, and get a good pair of horses."

"To take you to the railway, sir?"

"No, John, no—" and Mr. Newland faltered a little, "I don't think I'm quite equal to that. Four horses, John, four horses—we shall not lose much time—"

"Let me go up with you, sir," said Mr. Debenham, heartily. "You'll not be afraid of the rail with *me* by your side?"

"Yes, I shall—yes, I shall—what difference would that make? the boiler might blow us both up as well as one. No, no, no—there are some things I can do, and some I cannot. I can go to London in my own way, but not in yours."

They all felt this might be the case.

"So, John, you'll order four horses, and —John, I should like to *feel* the cushions when they're aired—Deborah can bring them to me; you'll have enough to do, my poor fellow." Then, turning to Mr. Debenham, "And if you, my good sir, will take a seat in my post-carriage, I'll be obliged to you; very much obliged, for I have lived so long out of the world that 1 may get confused. I believe London is not what it was. And I'm not quite what I was."

"I'll go, sir, with pleasure," said Mr. Debenham.

"So would I, sir," said Mr. Burrowes.

"No, Burrowes, no—two companions would be overpowering—I don't want a doctor—I feel I shall be supported. A lawyer I *may* want."

CHAPTER XII.

He whom a fool doth very wisely hit,
Doth very foolishly, although he smart,
Not to seem senseless of the bob.

AS YOU LIKE IT.

THE decision once made, nothing could exceed the despatch with which Mr. Newland carried it out. He would not hear of postponing his journey a single day.

" I may die, sir, I may die in the night, and then where are we all?" And when he was asked by Mr. Debenham what course he meant to pursue on arriving in London, he replied, "I will unfold that to you at leisure on the road. I have arranged my plan of operations, and believe I shall require no assistant, but simply a witness."

It was now between eleven and twelve o'clock, and as he had his toilette to make, his papers to put up, his lunch to antedate, and, very likely, his will to put where it would be most easily found, Eleanor, who felt her mission was accomplished, took leave of him. He raised her hands, one after the other, to his lips, bowing over them with the courtesy of a Grandison, and said,

"My dear young lady, according to the success or failure of my enterprise, I shall be accounted a *preux chevalier*, or a crazy Quixote; but never did knight-errant of old sally forth in a purer cause; and if I succeed, it will be mainly owing to you and your good mother."

He then, at her request, returned Mrs. Graydon's letter to her; saying the deposition would, with the papers he had already prepared, be sufficient.

Mrs. Debenham had found the half-hour a long one, yet it had been no more, when she saw her son and Eleanor, both looking very animated, issue from the gate of Stonewall; and a thought crossed her mind—" I wish those two were joined, not to be parted asunder." The next instant, Mr. Debenham handed Eleanor into the carriage, then sprang on his horse, and rode in advance of them, to reach his office as soon as possible, and make arrangements for his absence.

His horse, all in a heat, was being walked up and down when Mrs. Debenham and Eleanor reached the house.

" Well, mamma," said he, running in to them as soon as they entered, " I'm off this instant, for the impetuosity of young fellows like Mr. Newland brooks no delay. The distance is not so great but what I can soon run home, if I'm particularly wanted. Of

course Miss Graydon has told you everything—"

"Everything she *could* tell; but, my dear
Sam, what are you going to do? How long
shall you be away?"

"I know no more than you do. Good bye!
good bye."

"At any rate, write!"

"Yes, yes; I will!"

"Sam, Sam, stop! Have you put up everything you want? Have you had anything to
eat?"

"Yes, yes, cake and wine. Ned will carry
my valise to Stonewall. I'm going to take
him up with me. He'll be quicker running of
errands than that superannuated old boy of
Mr. Newland's."

Pressed as he was for time, he kissed his
hand to one and another as he rode through
the town, crying—

"I'm off to London with Mr. Newland!
We travel post, so look out for us."

No wonder, then, that the whole town turned out with as much alacrity to view the cortège as if Mr. Newland had been the Lama of Thibet.

> You would have thought the very windows spake,
> So many greedy looks of young and old
> Through casement darted their desiring eyes.

Mr. Newland's handsome, though old-fashioned post-chariot was speedily seen raising a cloud of dust in the distance; was speedily whirled over the noisy pavement of the High Street, by the four dashing bays, mostly used at weddings, with their postillions in yellow satin jackets and jockey-caps. In the rumble, enthroned in state, sat John, in all his glory, looking full ten years younger, now that he had shaved, and put on his best uniform. Within, through the plate-glass windows, were indistinctly discerned Mr. Newland and Mr. Debenham, in close conference. Ned, as outrider, rising prodigiously in his stirrups, closed the procession. Some one cried hurray ; and, by dint of repetition, they all hurrayed together, just as the turnpike-men

> Their gates wide open threw;

and the travellers dashed out of sight.

Eleanor and Mrs. Debenham had strained their eyes after them ; and now they returned to their own affairs. There succeeded a great lull ; which Eleanor was grateful for, as it enabled her to write more sheets than I care to specify to her mother and George. For, besides all that concerned Miss Clairvaux, had she not to tell Mrs. Graydon how unexpectedly Maurice had appeared on the stage, and excuse him as best she could ? The favourable impression he had made on the Debenhams was specially dwelt on, and, she hoped, would have its weight.

The next twenty-four hours were very flat, notwithstanding the variety afforded during the course of the day by calls from Mrs. Plover, Mrs. Rowe, and Miss Jones, who were all anxious to hear from headquarters the reason of this extraordinary journey to London. Mrs. Debenham began by being oracular, and ended by being explicit. Some extraordinary disclosures had taken place, in consequence of which everything would soon be put in proper train for Miss Clairvaux's release. Mr. Newland was the presiding genius of the business, and seemed endued with renewed health and energy for the express purpose. He had declared he would spare no effort or cost in carrying it through.

Mrs. Rowe and Miss Jones were sincerely glad; Mrs. Plover scarcely knew how to take it. What could those unexpected disclosures be? Was it permitted to ask?

Mrs. Debenham did not feel herself permitted to answer. Time would disclose. A very short time, she hoped and expected; but in the meanwhile, she was not at liberty to betray confidence. She did not think a more singular chain of events had occurred

since the affair of the Miss Offleys of Norton
Hall, except, indeed, in the particular of the
ghost, which some people did not believe in.
Mrs. Plover did not happen to have heard
about the ghost, nor about the Miss Offleys;
so Mrs. Debenham was happy to satisfy her
curiosity about a story that dated a hundred
years back, and related it as effectively as she
could.

But if the afternoon were flat, the evening
was especially so. Mrs. Debenham, who was
no reader, depended a good deal on chat for
her evening entertainment, failing which, or
a rubber, she usually took a nap. There were
a good many subjects in which she and
Eleanor might have found they had a common
interest, but somehow, they did not happen
to occur; or rather, the subject in hand
engrossed them too much for them to find
much interest in any other. At length Mrs.
Debenham begged for a little music. Eleanor
doubted if she really cared for it, but im-

mediately complied. At the end of the first
piece, Mrs. Debenham said, " That's a sweet
thing !"—at the end of the second, she was fast
asleep. With the praiseworthy view of pro-
longing her slumber, Eleanor played all the
lullaby-music she could think of—

"Ye spotted snakes with double tongue,"

and so forth. Finally, Mrs. Debenham, rous-
ing up, declared she had almost been asleep.

Next morning, her ruling doubt seemed to
be whether Sam would or would not write.
His letters were apt to be short, she said ;
but Sam, when he pleased, could write a very
good letter. (There were very few things
Sam could not do well, according to his
mother.)

The postman's knock, anxiously awaited,
was at length heard ; and Mrs. Debenham
uttered a joyous, triumphant exclamation at
the length of the letter when she opened it.
After running through a few lines, she
read aloud as follows :

"Clarendon Hotel.
Monday evening.

"Dear mamma,

"To dash up to London in the way we did, when we might have gone by rail, was more than respectable, it approached the sublime! As we were on the road, Mr. Newland, with surprising force and clearness, put before me all the evidence he had collected, and acquainted me with his projected course of action. His first object was to secure the best legal advice; his second, to see Mr. Foljambe. With regard to the first, I was of some use to him; and we decided on two or three legal names, to be tried in succession, if the first were not to be had.

"With regard to seeing Mr. Foljambe, I feared the poor old gentleman was preparing a disappointment for himself. Firstly, Mr. Foljambe would probably be, or pretend to be, out of town; second, if an interview were actually brought about, he would probably be too many for Mr. Newland.

"However, my remarks on this head met with no acceptance, and as I did not wish to press them in a discouraging way, we fell into silence. You know the great posting house called the Bunch of Grapes—Ned rode forward to bespeak a relay of horses; notwithstanding which, there was some delay in bringing them out: and as my brave-hearted old companion was beginning to feel a little worn, we alighted for a few minutes to stretch ourselves.

"Previous to this, while I had been musing on the Quixotism of our undertaking, and mentally comparing my doughty old friend to the Knight of La Mancha, I was a little startled to see what appeared to be a veritable Don Quixote, with helmet and lance, mounted on a respectable Rosinante, a little in advance. 'The days of chivalry are not past then, after all,' thought I, 'whatever

Burke may say to the contrary.' Passing
this remarkable figure, who exchanged
glances with the greatest sang-froid, we
presently came up with a group of the smallest piebald ponies I ever met; then a party
of horsemen, evidently Thespians, among
whom was a clown, riding with his face to
his poney's tail; and directly he caught my
eye, he stood upon his head. In short, we
had fallen in with the Circus people, with a
scout-patrol in advance. A waggon full of
properties and of women and children, drawn
by four horses, had already reached the
Bunch of Grapes, so that when we drove up,
they had to clear away a little. On my
observing to Mr. Newland that I believed
it was the company to which Toby Dick
belonged, he said, 'A happy coincidence;
pray look out for him—I should like to speak
to him in-doors;' and going into the hostelry,
he called for refreshments, for the good of
the house. Nothing was forthcoming but

bread, very good Cheshire cheese, and ale ;
which did not tempt him ; but I, being more
hungry, was less fastidious. Toby came in,
making all manner of antic congées, but
pulled a grave face when he saw Mr. Newland's serious aspect.

"While I ate bread and cheese, Mr.
Newland questioned him about his dining
with Miss Clairvaux on roast pork. Toby
declared there never was a greater falsehood ;
he never had eaten *with* her in his life, though
at her expense many times, from boyhood
upwards ; adding, ' She did say, one day, I
might have something to eat in the kitchen ;
and I remarked there was a beautiful little
loin of pork at the fire ; but she didn't
take the hint ! However, I had some cold
pie.' ' And told of it afterwards ?—' ' Maybe.' ' And said it was pork ?' ' Perhaps I
did.' ' And that you had partaken of it with
Miss Clairvaux ?' ' No, that I'll be bound I
didn't ! Sir, that must be one of Horsefield's

lies! Shouldn't I like to pummel his head!'
'Well, Toby, I should like to be able to
summon you on short notice, in case I have
to set you and him face to face.'

"While they were settling this, and after
Mr. Newland had taken a memorandum of
Toby's statement, which Toby signed with a
cross, and I witnessed, I stepped out to see
if the horses were changed, and caught a
glimpse of Horsefield, peering at us out of
the stable-yard. He hid away directly our
eyes met. I said to the landlord, 'how
comes that person here? What is he about?'
He said, 'He's waiting for a cast in a return
fly—he sleeps here sometimes.'

"Well, we only got one fresh pair of horses,
but by dint of promising the postillion an extra
fee, one of them engaged to go on with us
half a stage more, and we were content to
enter London in less dashing style. Just
as we were moving off, and the equestrians
were preparing to do the same, I heard

Horsefield making sneering remarks behind.
Toby, now on his poney, looked round, quick
as a bird; and, taking a half bitten apple from
his mouth, flung it with a will and with good
aim at Horsefield's eye! I could have roared
with laughter, especially as the clown, assum-
ing his professional whine, sang out, '*I*
didn't do it! *I* didn't do it! It slipped right
out of my hand! It slipped right out of my
hand!'

" Arrived in London, we drove at once to
——'s chambers, and, luckily, found him at
home; he had but just come up from Folkestone. There was no need for me to put in a
word—no one could have stated the case
better than Mr. Newland. —— took interest
in it; and gladly promised his best services,
in case they were needed. He had no great
faith in the visit to Mr. Foljambe, whom he
called clever but slippery. However, he said
he really had been out of town for a day
or two, at any rate, for he had seen

him at Folkestone, but he thought he
had returned now. So we drove to his
chambers, and there, by good luck, we caught
him !

"I think he knew us both by name. His
look said 'To what am I indebted for this
intrusion?' Mr. Newland proceeded to explain. As he proceeded, Mr. Foljambe's
countenance became darker and darker.
The violent effort by which he withheld his
temper from breaking forth was visible in the
deep, lurid red colour which gradually rose
even to his temples. In the most vigorously
controlled voice he said :

"'I distinctly deny your premises. I distinctly deny your right to interfere. Your
trouble is all in vain. I attend to you no
more than if I did not hear you. I shall not
even admit that I know where Miss Clairvaux is.'

"'I know that already, sir,' said Mr.
Newland, and he named the asylum and its

superintendent. Mr. Foljambe was evidently taken aback.

" 'And if you decline hearing me,' continued Mr. Newland, 'you will probably not decline hearing ——, who has already accepted my retainer.'

" ' What, what, what,'—he stammered, ' are you going to put yourself to all this foolish expense about, for the sake of a madwoman ?' ' Sir, that term applies not to Miss Clairvaux.' ' It *does*,' said he, vehemently, ' I could cite a thousand proofs.' ' Let me hear them, I am in no hurry.' ' But I am, if you are not ! This—why, I never heard anything so absurd in my life !' Mr. Newland made no reply, but eyed him severely.

" 'Oh, this is absolutely intolerable !' exclaimed he, starting up and walking about. ' To be bearded in my own office !—Sir, I have an appointment—I must go.' ' I, too, have an appointment, sir. I have promised to return to my counsel in the event of your refusing to adjust matters amicably. He will take immediate steps to bring it into court.' 'Why, you'll damage your own cause by it! You'll disgrace your client. There will be a complete exposure!' 'There will indeed be, and I do not wonder that you dread it.'

"Mr. Foljambe here snatched up his hat, as though he were going; but he remained a full half-hour after that. The conference continued to be very stormy. Mr. Newland never gave him the least advantage. He concluded it by saying in a determined manner, that the most rigid inquiry would be instituted into the particulars of Miss Clairvaux's seclusion, and urged very forcibly how much better it would be to repair her wrongs of his own accord, than to provoke an inquiry which would be attended with contention, anxiety, and perhaps obloquy. Mr. Foljambe appeared a little shaken, but did not commit himself, saying his time was

not his own.   Mr. Newland said, in that case,
we would wait on him to-morrow.

            "Your affectionate son,

                    "Samuel Debenham."

CHAPTER XIII.

Br.—When I spoke that, I was ill-tempered too.
Cas.—Do you confess so much? Give me your hand.

JULIUS CÆSAR.

How long seemed the twenty-four hours that had to pass before Mr. Debenham's next letter could arrive! A common interest in its contents drew Mrs. Debenham and Eleanor wonderfully close together, and strengthened the ripening friendship between them. The letter came in due course, and ran as follows:

"Clarendon, Tuesday night.

" My dear mother,

" I know that you and Miss Graydon will

be all impatience to hear the issue of our second conference. I have to apologise for concluding my last so abruptly; but paper failed.

"At the close of the first interview, Mr. Newland remarked to me, 'I am not disappointed with our progress thus far. It is something to have seen him, and to have got him to consent to see us again.' I own I did not think much had been done, though he seemed very well satisfied with his own proceedings. We came here, had an excellent dinner, and my old friend then retired to his room.

"This morning he breakfasted in bed. At ten he made his appearance, and announced himself ready to start. We found Mr. Foljambe apparently reading the Times. We had scarcely entered when he said, with hardly a shadow of courtesy, 'I really think it hardly worth while to go any farther into what you were speaking of yesterday. You have a theory of your own: I have facts. And they will bear me out.' 'Will you be kind enough to mention those facts?' said Mr. Newland, 'I hardly think it necessary,' said Mr. Foljambe, rustling his newspaper. '*I* think it quite necessary,' said Mr. Newland. 'However, if you prefer it, my lawyer shall apply for them in the proper manner.' '*Why* should you, a gentleman in years—put yourself thus out of the way in a matter that really does not in the least concern you?' 'Excuse me, an infringement of the liberty of the British subject concerns everybody.' 'An infringement of nonsense! this is downright meddling!' 'Sir, you are discourteous; but your want of temper shall not make me lose my own.' 'Temper has nothing to do with it.'—'Ah, my good friend,' said Mr. Newland temperately, 'temper has generally a great deal to do with cases of this kind. Possibly you and Miss Clairvaux have each been a little wanting in temper—

clever people often are; but when they cool, they should remedy their injustice.'

"'My good sir,' said Mr. Foljambe, throwing his newspaper on the floor, and addressing himself to the business in earnest, 'the statement of a few facts will, perhaps, undeceive you as to the nature of the case you have taken up. I only say perhaps; for it is very repugnant to us to abandon a hobby; especially when we ride it in the guise of a champion. Now, since you were here yesterday, I have learnt on good authority, that you have had the affliction of being confined to your own residence by infirm health for some years past: of course, all you have known of the affairs of the neighbourhood has been from hearsay, and many of them would not reach you at all.'

" A curious smile here played on Mr. Newland's face; but he only nodded his head a little, and said, 'may be so, may be so;' with covert irony however.

"Mr. Foljambe, encouraged by his seeming acquiescence, went on to say—'The lady in question, Alicia Clairvaux, has long been notorious for aberrations of mind—causeless bursts of joy and sorrow, immoderate flights of anger, eccentric predilections and aversions. I could cite two special instances; one, her absolute intolerance of a young man—'

"('Mr. Horsefield, perhaps,' said I, under my breath. He took no apparent notice.)

—'And another of her extravagant predilection for a young person of inferior condition whom she constantly has about her:'—

"'Ah, you mean Miss Graydon,' said Mr. Newland, quietly—'I know all about her; a most excellent and charming young lady.'— 'At present my guest,' added I, 'staying with my mother.'

"'Oh, well'—with a little shrug; 'what say you to her taking up a gang of Circus people, and actually giving the clown board and lodging!'

" ' *Now*, you come to a very remarkable chain of incidents indeed, sir,' said Mr Newland, cheerfully.—(' Remarkable? I should think so,' he muttered.) 'And I am very glad to be in a position to give you an outline of them exactly as they occurred, because I am sure they will interest you. Some mis-statements having got about, as they *will*, you know, in country places, this is the more desirable.'

" He then gave a brief and very clear statement of the whole affair, beginning with the ' feckless' character of the Dicks, and Miss Clairvaux's benevolent efforts to make something better of them, from Toby's boyhood upwards—then, his sudden disappearance; his return after a lapse of time with the Circus people—the fire, his leaping from the window with his father on his shoulders, and his being carried, in a shattered state, into her house.' Mr. Newland warmed as he spoke of the feeling it excited in the neighbourhood; and he openly mentioned the pleasure it had given him to send relief, through his medical man, to the poor people who had lost their furniture, 'which was all a poor invalid could do; but what was it, you know, to the personal cares of Miss Clairvaux and her young friend, who went about, binding up wounds and pouring in oil and wine? Sir, I see you feel this'—for Mr. Foljambe was evidently moved; 'and I like you all the better for it. You see, you and Miss Clairvaux are excellent persons both, but hitherto you have seen each other from imperfect and unfavourable points of view, like England and France.'

" 'Toby didn't, then, dine with her on pickled pork?' said Mr. Foljambe, trying to speak jocosely. 'I've his own deposition about that,' said Mr. Newland, pulling it out. ' By the merest chance in the world, or by the strangest Providence, we picked him up yesterday on the road.'

" Mr. Foljambe was silent. He took the deposition, ran through it and returned it.

'Of course I give up that,' said he. 'But the pains you have taken in getting up this case, is something astonishing!'

" 'You may say that, you may say that,' returned he complacently, 'but I haven't done yet. Many minor details—'

" 'Ah, but pardon me; however these trifles may seem to you to prove your case triumphantly, a fact that nullifies them all unfortunately remains behind. Miss Clairvaux's malady is hereditary.'

" 'Mother's or father's side?'

" 'On the side of her father, the Reverend Henry Clairvaux, a very excellent man, I believe.'

" And he went over the particulars of his death dispassionately enough, clearly believing in them himself. I observed him and Mr. Newland at this moment with great interest. Mr. Newland had altogether thrown over his line of conduct as a lawyer, and was acting entirely on his knowledge of and sympathy with human nature, greatly under the guidance of his own.

" 'Sir,' said he, having patiently heard him out, 'there is much to be said for the view you have taken of this, but I will now relate to you one of the most remarkable incidents that I remember ever to have heard of, since that which led to poor Henry Nugent Bell's securing the missing link in the evidence for the Huntingdon peerage, by jumping off a stage-coach into a poor market-woman's cart. You remember all about that, I dare say ?' 'Oh yes, very well.'

" Mr. Newland then, with the most attractive sweetness of demeanour, (why was not Vindex a special pleader ?) related all that you know so well already, Miss Graydon—I mean, mamma ; and as he proceeded, I saw Mr. Foljambe visibly interested, his finger and thumb nervously fillipping each other under the table.

" 'This is very extraordinary,' said he.

" ' Extraordinary? 1 see the finger of
Heaven in it,' said Mr. Newland. ' Here was
a little widow lady whom I had never before
set eyes on, who at the first word, started off,
not even to Staffordshire but to Cheshire, (for
I gave her the wrong county), to look up
friends she had completely lost sight of—these
friends were absolutely without information,
but they passed her on to people she had
never heard of, in the wilds of Staffordshire ;
and there, the very first evening, without even
a leading word, the mystery that had been
concealed for years, that nobody but the
speaker knew to exist, all came out ! he said
he felt himself ' impelled !' And he said he
could not rest till he had got a lawyer to take
his deposition ! My dear friend,' said Mr.
Newland rising, and benignly approaching
him, ' you could not be to blame for not
knowing these things, for nobody knew them
but this poor man and God ! But *now*,' continued he, looking full at him with those won-

derful eyes of his, 'you may say, *whereas I was blind, now I see !'*

"Mamma, *I* was blind, just then, for a moment, myself; and so, I fancy, was Mr. Foljambe. At any rate, I saw him the next instant wring Mr. Newland's hand, and then say, with rather an unsuccessful attempt to speak in his ordinary dry way—

"'Well, I should like, of course, to look over that deposition.'

"'Here it is,' said Mr. Newland, whipping it out, and trying, I think, not to be too eager.

"Mr. Foljambe read it attentively through; pausing once or twice, I believe, to arrange his own thoughts and resolutions on the whole business. At length, having ended it, he looked up and said in a manly way :—

"'This alters the whole affair. Miss Clairvaux shall be set free.'

"You may imagine our joy. I can't remember what was said, nor is there need. So

much better, as we observed, than bringing
it into court. Mr. Newland expressed a wish
that he, or I, should go to the asylum for
her, but he would not allow that. He said
he must take that on himself, and that as
the Bunch of Grapes was a half-way house
to both, she should meet us there to-morrow if we wished it.

"So to-morrow, dear mamma and Miss
Graydon, prepare for *La glorieusse rentrée*,
and

"Let the bells be rung and the mass be sung,
And the feast be eaten merrily!

"I think Foljambe had half a mind to ask
us to dine with him! Especially after my
whispering in his ear that the doughty old
champion was Vindex! He raised his eyebrows a little, and muttered 'oh, that ex-
plains'. Doubtless it was easier and pleasanter
to him to lower his lance before such a known
redresser of injuries. We drove strait to ——,

to tell him his services would not be wanted. He was as glad as we could expect him to be, but very much surprised at Foljambe's giving in. He said it was without precedent. Coming back here to lunch, I remarked to Mr. Newland that I hoped Mr. Foljambe would not take any advantage of us after all. He said 'if he does, we are but where we were; but I will not do him the wrong to suspect it.' 'He may let her out,' said I, 'on condition of her signing that paper first.' 'She would never come out on those terms, and I do not think he would do so badly: but even if he did, the shame would be his, the release hers.' 'And the loss,' I added. 'What is the loss of a little money,' he rejoined 'compared with that of liberty? Oh, money may be too dearly bought!'

"Well, after luncheon, the good old man went regularly to bed! nightcap and all! curtains drawn and shutters closed. (And rushlight lighted, I dare say.) He has gone through a good deal, poor old fellow. And I sallied out and saw everything, Since then, we have had a capital dinner; he is napping in his arm-chair, and I have killed time with the Browbeater and this letter, and am now going to the play. Tell the good news to all whom it may concern. *Au revoir*, ladies!

"Your faithful and trusty

"SAMUEL DEBENHAM.

"A capital cut-up of ladies' dresses in the Browbeater!"

It almost seemed too good to be true! Why, if all went as was expected, Miss Clairvaux would be amongst them in a few hours! *O gioja! O contento!*

"And the bells must be rung, my dear!" said Miss Debenham, taking her son's words literally, "and though the mass won't be sung, it is prayer-day, and we shall be just in time for church. Then I can speak about

the bells, and tell the good tidings to Dr.
Hurst and other friends as we come out,
according to Sam's wish."

Eleanor had never felt more ready to go to
mornfng service. It was the 24th day
of the month, when the morning psalms are
so full of thanksgiving. And fervently and
gratefully did she join in them ; but while the
lessons were being read, she could not help
thinking of Miss Clairvaux. Just in the
stillness at the close of the second lesson, the
church door creaked, and then closed with a
hollow sound, and some late comer came in
with light pit-pat steps. Eleanor looked
absently up ; it was her mother ! Their eyes
gladly met ; and, the next instant, they were
side-by-side, exchanging a tender squeeze of
the hand.

After the service, Mrs. Debenham was in
all her glory ; speaking to the bell-ringer, the
rector, and a knot of chosen friends, while
Eleanor walked back with her mother. The

rector read the letter aloud to them in the vestry. Then they all scattered to spread the news about the town; and though ill news flies fast, good news sometimes flies faster. It was determined, in literal accordance with Mr. Debenham's injunction, to let the reception be as public as possible; and as the time of the *glorieuse rentrée* was quite uncertain, the rector amused himself by supplying the want of a warder with a sounding horn by relays of small boys, who were to hurray as soon as the post-chariot was descried in the distance. Largesse of halfpence and gooseberries being at the same time distributed, they employed the half-holiday in eating the latter, and playing pitch-and-toss with the former. At every cloud of dust, they cried, "here they come!" so that a good many hurras were raised before the right time came.

Meanwhile, Eleanor, after a joyful dialogue with her mother, left her reading Mr. Debenham's letters, while she ran down to the green lane, to tell the good news to Claudia. It was uncertain whether the old woman at the Peaked House would have received any notice to quit; so Eleanor went there in the next place, accompanied by Claudia, to see how matters stood. Just at the turn of the road, she came suddenly on Mr. Horsefield, with an eye like a half-ripe plum. He looked excessively annoyed at seeing her, or rather at her seeing him; and taking a short cut across the grass, which the heat had made extremely slippery, he slid a yard or two, and narrowly escaped falling.

Eleanor found the old woman tying up her bundle, and Fly scampering about in frantic excitement.

" Mr. Horsefield's been, miss, and taken all the seals off the doors," said the old châtelaine. " So I'm quite ready to go, directly there's anybody to leave in charge."

" I'm here to take charge," said Claudia; alertly; " and I shall begin by setting open all the doors and windows, for the house smells as musty as ever it can do; and oh, my goodness! the carpets faded like anything for want of drawing down the blinds before the doors were locked. And I don't believe the stair-carpets have been taken up, nor the rods rubbed since we left. And as for the floors!—"

"A likely thing I was going to scrub another person's floors," grumbled the old lady, "when I was allowed neither soap or flannel. But there, I leave no friends behind me, nor have ever had any valley set upon me; which is hard, considering the life I've led. However, I must be off without more words, or I shall lose the train. Good bye, miss."

And curtseying civilly to Eleanor, she went away, without any leave-taking of Claudia, who looked after her in a disdainful manner.

"I must give a general clean-up to-day, and begin scouring to-morrow," said she.

"I hope Hester will come back by that time. They say, ' when the cat's away, the mice will play'—I don't know how it's been with others, miss, but I've been and got engaged to be married!"

CHAPTER XIV.

A man should never be ashamed of owning he has been in the wrong; which is but saying in other words that he is wiser to-day than he was yesterday.

"Hark! there are the boys hurraing," cried Eleanor.

And so they were; but it was only one of their false alarms. Claudia set to her work with dust-pan and brush, but Eleanor, who had mounted the bank commanding the roads, saw some one coming quickly towards her, whose violet stockings proclaimed him to be Maurice.

"I was beginning to wonder what had become of you," said she, "and should have wondered more, had I not had so many other things to think about."

"I went to see Aunt Jane. She's a good old soul, you know, and she would not part from me in a hurry. When 1 came away, she gave me twenty pounds. 'To buy a Christian suit of clothes,' she was pleased to say; but I know she liked my toggery. I would be happy to oblige her if I knew what the early Christians wore. A toga, I suppose, or something of that sort. Afterwards, I looked up George, and we had some famous talks. He told me about all that has been going on here; and so, you see, I shall get a glimpse of Miss Clairvaux after all."

"If all goes according to our hopes; but how late it is getting."

"That's right! Make yourself miserable. Ladies love to do so. Nice and grateful they are, for all their mercies and blessings!"

"No, I am not going to make myself miserable, I am very, very happy; only a little anxious. Mamma is here; you must see her."

"I have seen her already. Of course, I went first to Mrs. Debenham's; expecting to find you there; instead of which, I found mamma. What a wonderful woman! What spirit she has shown! How well she looks! I did not see Mrs. Debenham; she was out, Mrs. Graydon said, telling everybody about Miss Clairvaux, and advising them to drink the sweet and eat the fat, and send portions to them for whom nothing was prepared. George and I went to the play last night. There we saw Mr. Debenham. It did me good to see how he was enjoying it. It was an English opera; the music was wretched —such as I could compose, to any amount, at any given time; but how he was enjoying it! We did not disturb him. George would have liked to come down with me. He hopes

Mrs. Graydon will return home soon. He says the Marchioness has only two ideas: mutton-chops and pork-chops."

Then, with a groan,

"Oh, Eleanor! My time here is very short. I must start off to-morrow."

At this instant, the bells began ringing with such clangour as to drown the treble hurrays in the offing; and Maurice, catching Eleanor's hand, ran with her down the lane. All the people were at their doors or wide-open windows; everybody's head was turned towards the direction in which the regular tramp of four horses was heard nearer and yet more near. The loud, deep bass of men's voices was heard in a hearty cheer as the post-carriage dashed along the High Street, with Mr. Newland in it, bowing right and left; and, beside him, Miss Clairvaux, with her veil down.

Mr. Debenham, mounted on his own horse, which his groom had ridden to town, gal-

lopped beside them. They paused for a single
instant at Mr. Debenham's door, to inquire
if the Peaked House were ready; and Mr.
Debenham threw himself from his horse to
press Miss Clairvaux to alight, while his
mother and Mrs. Graydon stood upon the
steps; but, in stifled accents she declined,
and the horses wheeled round and drove
down a narrow side-street to her home.

Directly Eleanor saw this manœuvre, she
said hastily to Maurice,

"The scene is too much for her. She is
overcome by it, and wants to be alone. I
will run back, but you had better not come
with me."

He was disappointed, but nodded acquiescence, and she darted off, and by crossing
the undulating ground, reached the gate before the carriage could. Mr. Burrowes was
there before her. He said heartily to Mr.
Newland as they drew up,

"I'm sure, sir, you must be gratified by your success!"

Mr. Newland threw up his hand and said,

"This is worth living for!" He then alighted, and handed out Miss Clairvaux, who went in without looking up or saying a word; beckoned Eleanor to him, and kissed her with the affection of a parent, then signed to Mr. Burrowes to follow him into his carriage, and drove off with him. Eleanor hastily re-entered the Peaked House.

Both the maids, looking rather awe-stricken, stood in the little hall. Miss Clairvaux had spoken kindly to each of them in passing, and was now in the dining-room. She was standing, without her bonnet, leaning against the table, in the same steel-coloured silk dress in which Eleanor had first seen her—the dress in which she had been taken away. Usually she wore caps, but at this moment she had none; and her glossy, abundant, dark-brown hair, streaked though it was with much more grey, was wound up in a simple coil, after being lifted in sweeping bands from a little below her ears, so as to shew the beautiful form of her head.

She was sallow, thin, and looked very melancholy; but was very calm and composed. She held out her arms to Eleanor, and kissed her many times. Eleanor shed a few tears.

"There is no one in the house, I hope, except ourselves?" said Miss Clairvaux. "No? I am glad to hear it. How quiet the old place looks! We will have our tea here, Claudia, for the present. I don't want to go into the other room. Where is your mother, Eleanor?"

"At Mrs. Debenham's."

"She can come and sleep here to-night, with you. I shall like to see her." Then, rather abruptly—

"Let us pray."

She dropped on her knees; her head resting

on her arms against the dining-table. The maids, crying a little, knelt too, as did Eleanor. But not a word was uttered. Presently, with a deep sigh, she arose.

"Thank God. I am sure you have all thanked God. I shall thank Him for ever and ever. Such wonderful friends !—"

Then she went up into her bed-room, and shut herself in. Eleanor, with tearful eyes, wrote a pencilled note to her mother; begging her to come to the Peaked House. In a little while, Mrs. Graydon arrived, and they had a quiet talk together, straying round the little garden, with hands on each other's shoulder. It was a lovely summer evening. The bells had ceased ringing, and, as the old song says :—

Every leaf was at rest, and they heard not a sound,
Save the woodpecker tapping the hollow beech tree.

Looking up at Miss Clairvaux's window, they saw her looking tranquilly down upon them, resting her cheek upon her hand. She nodded, and smiled.

"You look so comfortable together," she said. "I shall come down to tea directly. We will have tea early, for I am very thirsty; and so, I dare say, are you."

How sweet it was to hear her dear voice! Mrs. Graydon had brought a basket of beautiful hot-house fruit; and Eleanor gathered some flowers to set it out with for the tea-table. This was a favourite task of hers, for which she had a special genius. Claudia had obtained from one quarter or another, everything a tea-table could want; so that when the loud hissing urn was brought in, and the tea bell rang, Miss Clairvaux came down to as inviting a spread as ever an epicure could have wished for.

"Oh, this is comfortable!" she said, with pleasure; and then she kissed Mrs. Graydon.

"Really, we only want your son George."

" George would be very glad to be here, if he were not watching a case; but I think you would have found him rather in the way."

" On the contrary, I should have been glad; for I feel a little—lonely, and should like very well to have a man in the house. Just for a night, you know. It is very foolish."

" I know a young man who might answer the purpose as well as George," said Mrs. Graydon.

" Mamma!"—interrupted Eleanor; but Mrs. Graydon went on :—

" Do you remember, Miss Clairvaux, a talk I had with you at Easter, about a certain Maurice Day?"

" Yes, quite well," said Miss Clairvaux, smiling in her old pleasant way.

" Well, this naughty fellow has come from Rome without leave, to satisfy himself that Eleanor is alive and well, and faithful, and so forth. They have had the pleasure of seeing one another at Mrs. Debenham's; but he is going away to-morrow; and—why, there he is, to be sure!"

In fact, Mr. Maurice's good-looking person was seen, by accident of course, straying across the turfy undulations, sketch-book in hand, and looking leisurely about him with the air of a stranger. Suddenly, a good point strikes him; he is sketching with all his might.

"Let him come in by all means," said Miss Clairvaux quickly. "Run out to him, Eleanor."

Eleanor joyfully obeyed, and in her absence, Miss Clairvaux expressed strongly to Mrs. Graydon the pleasure it would give her to make acquaintance with the young man, and to do everything in her power to promote his and Eleanor's mutual happiness.

This desire was certainly not lessened upon acquaintance. The evening passed very calmly and cheerfully to them all; and when prayer-time came, Miss Clairvaux officiated as usual; saying, as she laid her hand affectionately on the Bible,

"During my absence from you—which seemed longer than it was—this Book was my greatest friend!"

CHAPTER XV.

Haply, the seas, and countries different
With variable objects, shall expel
This something-settled matter in her heart.

THIS was the only allusion she had made to what had passed ; or if, during her tête-à-tête journey with Mr. Newland, she had revealed anything to him, it was known only to themselves ; he respected and therefore deserved a woman's confidence.

Nobody in Meadowleigh had supposed it possible her lips would be sealed to them. Showers of cards poured in on her the next day; tokens of respect, and of curiosity desirous to be fed. It was left to die a natural death. Eleanor made her rounds a few days afterwards, with Miss Clairvaux's kind regards and warm thanks for her neighbours' sympathy. They would make allowance for her wishing to quiet her nerves, and banish all remembrance of a disagreeable episode in her quiet life, which had originated in a mistake.

Mrs. Plover repeated "mistake," and "nerves," among her select acquaintance with marked irony, but found them willing to accept the words in their simple significance, and show their real kindness by believing Miss Clairvaux to mean what she said.

To Mrs. Graydon and Eleanor, however, she spoke with the openness they deserved; though she owned that the subject was so painful to her that she wished to dwell on it as little as she possibly could. She said so to them in her own bed-room, the very first night after her return.

"What poor creatures we are," said she, "that cannot even bear the weight of our own gratified wishes! Jane Taylor says somewhere, that a severer punishment could hardly be invented for young people, than the infliction on them of some of the out-of-the-way things they desire for themselves. As a young person, I had a great fancy to see and judge for myself of the routine of an asylum. In later years, I should almost have decided the penalty of a short stay in one, not too great to pay for the opportunity of ascertaining abuses, and perhaps devising remedies. I know all about it now. There is a great deal to be said on both sides. I am convinced that no human being ought to have the irresponsible charge of others. Temper, love of power, natural hardness, great and sudden provocations, and total misconceptions of cases, render them liable to sad abuses. I say so as regards the unhappy persons who really require restraint; but when they do *not*, the offence is loud and cries to heaven! I told Jasper Foljambe so, but without any vindictiveness. He had become so fully aware that temper and self-interest had blinded him, and brought him to the verge of a great crime, that he acknowledged himself wrong, and even named compensation. But I told him, (quite calmly, you know,) that nothing could compensate to me for the past, and I would rather forgive him for it out of hand, and forget the great wrong he had done me as soon as I could.

"And that's what I mean to do," added she, deeply sighing. "There is great sweetness, great peace, in forgiving, when we don't do it in a vile, grandiose sort of way, that is no forgiveness at all, in fact. And after all, I was not there so very long; only the worst was, that I did not know when I should come out! That was one of the worries we make for ourselves. A bird does not like being caged; but he does not trouble himself with thinking

'I wonder if I shall ever get out?' And there were some poor creatures, too, to whom I could minister—so much worse off than I was! They grew fond of me; but then we were separated, which I thought and still think was very hard, and unnecessary. However, my enforced seclusion gave me time to chew the cud of many bitter things I should never have dwelt on of my own accord. Well—' man proposes, God disposes.' Had it not been for you, my dear, dear friends, I should be there still. I am very glad I am not. How pleasant it is to be in this dear room again. Mrs. Graydon, here is my mother's miniature—have I ever shown it you?"

She *had* shown it to her; but Mrs. Graydon looked at it again! and at Mr. Clairvaux's likeness, and silhouettes of some of her dead brothers and sisters, and then they kissed one another with loving words, and went to bed.

How she and Mr. Foljambe had settled

their money-matters, I know no more than
you do. They had no more disputes, and
Mr. Horsefield's face was no more seen
in the neighbourhood.

To the Debenhams and Mr. Burrowes,
Miss Clairvaux was more cordial than before,
for she felt deeply grateful to them; but
they respected her wishes, and did not intrude on her confidence. Her manner was
calmer and certainly sadder than before; she
was more and equable less entertaining.

Mrs. Graydon and Maurice had arranged
to go to London together. But before she
started, she went by appointment to Stonewall, to take leave of Mr. Newland, who had
fallen back pretty much into his old habits.
When she entered and saw the good old
gentleman airing his pockethandkerchief before a fire, for which a damp day afforded
his excuse, though in the midst of summer,
she could not help thinking what an effort
his journey must have been to him, and ap-

preciating his self-denial accordingly. A fine picture by Leslie, of Don Quixote reading in his study, seemed emblematic of one phase in his own character; its pendant, by the same delightful artist, was Sir Roger de Coverley in his picture gallery. A sympathy with both these characters had probably actuated his choice.

On her inquiring how he felt, he replied in the minor key, which presently changed into the major —

"A little reaction, my good madam, a little reaction. But I would not cancel the last week's work, for a thousand aches and pains!—nor, I'll answer for it, would you."

"Oh no, sir!"

"And how is our dear Miss Clairvaux?"

"Very calm and quiet, sir. Very thankful to all who have helped her."

"Very natural to her generous nature; but we should have been brutes, my dear madam, if we had done less—we should have been brutes. You and your daughter, my dear lady, are of those who, as St. Paul says, ' *by reason of use*, have their senses exercised to discern both good and evil.' Yes—you have not let your excellent natural endowments lie dormant, for want of use; and the child is the pattern of the mother—none of your puling misses that cry over a tale of sickly sentiment, and leave their friends and fellow-creatures to shift as they can. I detest lymphatic temperaments, madam, for my part! It is the dry weather that produces least bran and most meal in the grain! You and your daughter are all meal and no bran. And now, you are going away, I suppose, and I shall lose sight of you. I shall relapse into my old habits, which secure me liberty and happiness, and exclude company as rigidly as ever. To you and yours, however, and to Miss Clairvaux, my doors shall always be open; if you give me due notice, that is; if you give me reasonable notice. But an

old man must have time to change his slippers; yes, an old man should have time
given him to change his slippers. And now,
about your children. You have a son, I
understand. What is he doing?"

"Indeed, sir, I am rather anxious about
him. He has just completed his medical
education, and is waiting for an opening."

"Well, well, but there are plenty of open-
ings. As assistant, or partner, or what?"

" Oh, he has no money to buy a partnership—he will gladly be an assistant—"

" In a country place? Like this, for
instance?"

" Oh yes, sir! He prefers the country."

" Why, there's Mr. Burrowes, hard up for
an assistant at this moment!—breaking down,
my dear madam, under too much work!—
and would not object to a partner. I'll tell
you what, my dear madam. At a word from
me, Burrowes will take your son on trial, as
assistant; and if he finds him capable and

well-conducted, he and I will settle hereafter about the partnership, without putting you to inconvenience."

Mrs. Graydon pressed her hands closely together. For the moment, she could not speak.

" Not a word ! or you'll pain me," said he, holding up his finger at her. " Everything must depend on the young man himself. Capability, integrity, must be the foundation-stones of every man's success in life ; but the medical man must have yet another, which no man had better want—gentlemanly ad-dress. It is a great thing in every walk of life ; it is a *sine qua non* to the medical man ; in spite of Abernethy's bearishness It would not do again. Would not go down, my dear lady ; should not and would not. What is your son about now, do you say ?"

" Sitting up every night, sir, with a lady in brain fever, brought on by reading sensation-novels in nonpareil type—the third case in six weeks."

" What, what ? Sensation-novels in non-pareil type? Let me book it, my good lady —let me book it. Such a treacherous memory is mine."

Then, when he had noted it,

" Well, but about my young favourite, Miss Eleanor. What of her future? Is she going to continue with Miss Clair-vaux ?"

" For the present, sir, at any rate."

" Is Miss Clairvaux likely to discharge her? perhaps she is not quite equal to the expense—"

" Oh no, sir, it is not that—in fact, Eleanor is engaged to be married."

" Oho! Who's the happy man? One of our Meadowleigh swains?"

" Oh no, sir. Eleanor was engaged, so to say, (only her father would not let it be called an engagement) some time before she came into this neighbourhood; to a pupil of Mr. Graydon's, a young artist."

"Talking of artists, I've heard of a young fellow in a whimsical dress, who has been seen sketching in this neighbourhood."

"That is the young man, sir," said Mrs. Graydon, smiling; and she gave a little sketch of his antecedents, and mentioned traits in his character which could not fail to prepossess Mr. Newland in his favour.

"Well, well, well," said he, "I should like to have a look at this young fellow; just out of curiosity, you know, out of pure curiosity. But it won't do to tell him that— no, no, that would never do! Let me think how it can be managed. Tell him I want his opinion whether a picture in my possession is a genuine Mieris or not, and that I have two good Leslies, and a Raphael portfolio which he can see at the same time: or, stay —would he take it amiss, think you, if I commissioned him to make me a crayon study of Miss Graydon?"

"Surely not," said Mrs. Graydon, laughing. "You could hardly have devised anything he would like so much."

"Miss Clairvaux too, perhaps—I should exceedingly value a likeness of Miss Clairvaux."

"I doubt, though, her consenting to sit. And Maurice's stay here will be short—"

"Well, send him over, send him over. A crayon head or two will not take him long. I want to see his method of handling. He will find me at his service any time during the afternoon. By that time I shall have dashed off a few lines to shew up an anonymous scribbler, who has dared to assert in this morning's paper, that, of all impostors, our missionaries are the worst, and that they will tell lies to any amount as long as they can continue to gull a maudlin public. He must have a trouncing, madam; a thorough trouncing."

"Indeed, sir, I think he deserves it; and I hope he will see your remarks!"

On her return to the Peaked House, where Maurice was completely absorbing Miss Clairvaux with "what we do at Rome," Mrs. Graydon told him of Mr. Newland's desire to see him, and urged his compliance so strenuously, that Maurice, to whom the outworks of Stone·wall were already familiar, hastened to induct himself into an inky suit of solemn black, to fit himself for the old gentleman's levée. Either they found they liked each other by the rule of contrary, or they discovered some mutual taste which drew them together, for the interview was a pleasant and prolonged one. Strange to say, Maurice and Mrs. Graydon found they could spend a few more days at Meadowleigh; and during that interval, he produced excellent heads of Eleanor and Miss Clairvaux, as L'Allegra and La Pensierosa. The weather was now very sultry, and it was discovered that they could all enjoy themselves most in the garden; Maurice making studies, *al fresco*, of his sitters, while Mrs. Graydon rifled the raspberry canes for each of them in turn.

It was very pleasant! and Miss Clairvaux thought it well worth while to sit for her likeness, to gratify her kind friend, Mr. Newland, and bring Maurice into the way of his patronage. So successful were Maurice's studies, that Mr. Newland, who had only suggested them as tests, saw what was in him, and actually commissioned a historical picture for two hundred guineas!

Oh, how much there was for them all to discuss, in the choice of a subject; and how many books were hunted over, and how many passages read, and how many visits were paid to Stonewall! Mr. Debenham found his way, one morning, into Miss Clairvaux's garden; and discoveved it to be an excellent lounge; too excellent for a business man to indulge in, more than once in a way. And he gave

Maurice no pretext for fancying him a rival, for he took lively interest in his engagement, and asked him, at what he thought an opportune moment, when it was likely to come off!

It really was time now for Maurice to be on his way back to Rome; he was joyous, grateful, and hopeful; full of high resolve and virtuous endeavour.

"Oh that you were coming too!" exclaimed he. "Why should not you winter in Rome, Miss Clairvaux?"

Miss Clairvaux actually changed colour.

"It has been the dream of my life!" said she; "and I know not why it should not now be accomplished. I do not settle down here as I ought, now that I have been so roughly disturbed. My rest is broken by troubled images. I should like very well to take Eleanor abroad with me, if you would take care of us, and see that we were not imposed upon. The chief question is about this house.

—I don't care to let it, and have my household properties desecrated by strangers, even if a tenant were sure to be forthcoming. Oh! but George Graydon is coming to Meadowleigh! and his mother will naturally like to be with him. She shall keep house for him here till our return."

"Oh, delightful!" exclaimed Eleanor.

For Mr. Burrowes' pressing need of an assistant brooked no delay, and Mr. Newland had given him such weighty reasons for making trial of George, that he had entered into treaty with him; and Mrs. Graydon, without waiting any longer for Maurice, had gone home to explain, advise, and accelerate. So, as soon as Mrs. Graydon's consent to the arrangement had been asked and obtained, Maurice was empowered to make the necessary preparations for the journey. We know enough of Miss Clairvaux's circumstances to be sure it was going to be conducted on economical principles; for people can't fly here and there about the world without its costing something—unless, say, to France and back in twelve hours as an excursionist. Still, when you go prudently to work, you may do a good deal and cover many miles at little more expense than living at home ; but then you must not aspire to milord it like the Dorrits with their retinue, but content yourself with quietly seeing all that is best worth seeing, and receiving as many new impressions, and reviving as many old associations as you can for your money. Now, it is certain that, in this point of view, the Rialto and Bridge of Sighs would be a better bargain to Miss Clairvaux than to Mr. Dorrit ; and in a general way it may be said, that the heavier crops we reap from others' minds and our own at the beginning, the cheaper we find it in the end.

Besides, apart from poetical associations, and all the treasures of art, there was something to be seen and inquired about in Italy, very dear to Miss Clairvaux's heart. The kingdom of Italy was no longer a sealed country; she knew from reading the Times, that twenty thousand Bibles were already circulating in it, and twenty-three thousand pupils in the ex-kingdom of Naples alone were receiving elementary education in the schools; some of them running a mile to them in the evening, after a hard day's work. She had interested herself in them afar off, and she wanted to see some of them on the spot. Her destination, however, was not to the free states, but to benighted Rome; the old city that stands on a volcano, which makes its heat felt through the region round about and gives it its very name, the Solfaterra. She would like to see and study it, while it could be done; who should say that Rome would ever be purified, except in death?

Mrs. Graydon was delighted with the Italian scheme, it would be so good for Maurice, so charming for Eleanor; and (last, certainly, in the mother's heart) such a restorative to Miss Clairvaux. She was most thankful, too, for the offer of the Peaked House; the only question was, what to do with her own. To let it furnished would be the best plan, if possible; but houses so often refused provokingly to be let when people wanted to get rid of them, unless they happened to be in very attractive situations.

George was instrumental in helping her out of this difficulty, which he made his own, as it was for his benefit that the move was to take place. The gentleman with the gimlet in his head (Curtis was his name) was still always complaining. He had undertaken to produce, in a given time, a work on the great sewerage question, thrown into the form of a domestic novel in blank verse. On casting up the amount of copy he had prepared, it fell short of the stipulated measure by thirty thousand words. Here was a pretty state of things! It was no good to say to him, " you must write some more." Curtis's head was like a bottle, and Curtis had poured all the contents out. You might squeeze the bottle and break it, but it would yield no more disinfecting fluid. In despair he seized the pen, but the gimlet threatened to set to work again, accompanied by the humming of a dozen peg-tops. To add to his wretchedness, there were hand-organs beneath his window and a cornupœon player in the distance. George chanced to look in and found him nearly distracted.

"Take me and bury me," said Curtis, "and put Miserrimus on my tombstone."

"What's the matter?" said George, "what, still at your thirty thousand words? why, that is but three thousand lines! you may knock them off in no time."

"They'll knock me off, I think."

"Pooh, pooh. I'd sit down and help you, only, unfortunately, I'm not up in the subject."

"I've fully developed it."

"Very well, then if you only want to cover

paper, there are three ways—dress, scenery, and moral observations. Women always like to read about finery; the other two are easily skipped. So, there you are, you know!"

Mr. Curtis, however, having something like a conscience, objected to this imposition on a generous public. "And really," said he, "I think I might do something to the purpose if it were not for those horrid street-minstrels, and if you pay them off, they only come back again, like the Goths into Italy."

"Talking of Italy," says George, "my sister is going there, and my mother and I are going into the country. That's what you want, my dear fellow, country lodgings."

"Yes, but want must be my master," rejoins Curtis, almost whimpering, "for I can't manage to be more than a walk from the Bank. Everybody is going to have pleasure, I think, but my wretched self."

"Camberwell is but a walk from the Bank, and take it easy," says George; "and if you

like to have our little place, you may have it
for a mere song."

"Do you really mean what you say?" said
Curtis, letting go his beard. "No hand-
organs?"

"Oh no; or if one by chance now and
then, there's a front garden-gate you may lock."

"No practising young lady next door?"

"No young ladies or babies."

"Well, this seems attractive," said Curtis,
beginning to smooth his roughened hair
caressingly. "Only perhaps the terms—"

"Can't be more moderate. What do you
pay here?"

Curtis told him.

"You don't say so! What, for these two
rooms! Oh, my goodness, how you've been
imposed upon! Why, you may have our
house for that, piano and all. We shall only
take our clothes."

"In that case," said Curtis, brightening,
"I might have my sister to stay with me."

"Just so. My mother and I go out; your sister and you come in."

Now, in making this arrangement, and clenching it on the spot, the good-natured George knew he was letting his friend have a cheap bargain—it may be said, at Mrs. Graydon's expense. But he knew his mother so well, that he was quite sure he might do it. And Providence had showered such good things on them lately, that he wanted to do others good too.

With this general move, all the way round, there was little need to say more than " pair as you go out," as the clergyman at Liverpool did after marrying several couples with one reading of the service. And as Claudia was going to marry William Ford, Mrs. Graydon's little maid could take service under Hester, and be all the better and happier for the promotion.

Be it observed in a parenthesis, for the benefit of his brethren, that Mr. Curtis's removal from the Borough to Camberwell was attended with the happiest consequences. For two days he was aground. On the third day or rather evening, returned from some regular occupation which happily for himself, did not depend on the will of the moment, and finding himself in comfort and quiet, all at once the genial power began to exercise itself upon him. The whole plan of his task stretched out before him, as it once did to Robert Pollok, and has done to many another; so that at one glance he saw through it from end to end like an avenue. This is what, in writers, is commonly called inspiration; and truly, there is no better word; only it does not do to fancy it, or to depend on it. We will suppose the subject of Mr. Curtis's work to have been rather less ridiculous than was stated.

September's hues are on the trees, and Mr. Debenham is bagging many partridges. George wishes he had time for it; but on the whole, thinks it jollier to be in full practice, riding about the country on a good horse, popping in and out of fine old country seats ; sunning in the smiles of pretty girls and their mammas, and extorting many a laugh from gouty old gentlemen. Now and then he gets an invitation to dinner, sometimes to tea. Not a kettle-drum *before* dinner, mark you— an invention that had not yet reached Meadowleigh—but a severe tea of the substantial sort. And though the night-bell sometimes calls him out of his bed into the cold and the dark, it is all in the way of business, and he is rather proud of it.

Mr. Burrowes did not choose to give up to him his lunches at Stonewall, yet now and then Mr. Newland insisted on having "the young man," as he called him, sent to him, and protested afterwards that he found nothing amiss in his manners. "The old school and the new school, you know, Burrowes, are not alike—any more than the

Venetian and the Flemish; but both have their values."

One morning, George was sent for in a great hurry, and found the old gentleman in bed, in great trepidation.

"Can you cup, Graydon? Can you cup?"

"Oh yes, sir. It's nothing but a slap, and all the pain's over. I've brought my glasses; but I hope you won't want them. What's the matter?"

"I hardly know, Graydon. Something has given way in my head—something has given way."

"Any pain, sir?"

"None whatever. I had not been exerting myself in the least. Went to bed with my brain quite quiet. Slept all night—woke rather late—or rather was awakened by what took place in my head. A most extraordinary noise."

"Well, sir, suppose we keep quiet, till this extraordinary noise takes place again."

"No, no, no—not for the world. I could not bear it, sir! I could not bear it! I'm all in a tremble at the mere thought,"—(which was true enough.)

"Or, at least, wait till you have seen Mr. Burrowes, sir—"

"No, no, I won't see Burrowes," (very testily) "he'll be all for temporizing. No half-measures, Graydon. No time should be lost."

"Well, sir, it's rather a responsibility, as the King of France's surgeon said when he drew the blood-royal. You're old, you see; and I'm young, you see—"

"And therefore should obey orders, Mr. Doctor."

"Oh yes, sir—just so." And George began to make a great jingling with his glasses, and shake out towels; spreading them carefully at right angles, as if for an incantation, or mathematical demonstration.

"Can you tell me what o'clock it is, sir?"

(in the faint hope that Mr. Burrowes would soon pay his daily call.)

" Have not you a watch, my young friend ?"

" Yes, sir, only it won't go, unless I carry it."

" Humph.   Well, you'll find my watch on that table."

" No, sir," after occupying about five minutes in every likely and unlikely place. " Can't say I either see it or hear it."

" Oh, here it is, under my pillow."   And he feebly held it towards him, without so much as opening his eyes.

" Why, sir, the spring's broken ! Why, sir ! the ——"

George was going to explode with laughter, but with immense presence of mind controlled himself, as he saw the colour mount into the old gentleman's face as vividly as if he had been a girl.

" What, what ?" stammered he, " was it only the chain running down ?   Heaven be praised, Graydon! It really sounded as if it were inside my head! I was half asleep, you know, and had had troubled dreams, I believe, and so—"

"Oh, yes, sir, it's as simple as possible."

"Makes *me* look rather simple though, Graydon? monstrously simple—"

"My dear sir—"

"Not a word—don't let's us talk of it any more. I hate to think of it. Graydon, my dear fellow, don't shew me up for an old noodle! Don't let Burrowes hear of it! He's such a——"

"Honour bright, sir! I'll clear away all these things before he comes."

"Do, do, do!—and carry them away with you as fast as you can! And put that rascally old repeater into the bag too—"

"Sir! why, it's worth—"

"Never you mind what it's worth. In the first place, you don't know. And, at all events,

I can never bear to see it again. So, if you can get the chain mended—"

" Of course I can, sir, but really—"

" No words, I tell you, no words—Graydon, you're a capital fellow! Very likely I shall tell all about it to Burrowes myself, some day, but at my own time, you know ; at my own time. Well, be off with you now, as soon as you can, or he'll find you here and see the bag! I shall get up now and—"

" I really think, after the shock you have had, you had better keep a little quiet —"

" Shock? Stuff and nonsense! I'm shocked when I think of it! I shall get up, I promise you, have a cup of good beef-tea, and do a little writing. *That* will quiet my nerves, sir !"

George never took so much credit to himself as for keeping his countenance during this scene. It was of substantial benefit to him ; for his self-command and humane good-nature were keenly felt by Mr. Newland, who thereafter thought he could never do too much for him. At first he kept his own counsel respecting the watch-chain; but, finding Mr. Burrowes a little jealous of his junior's patronage and petting, he relieved his mind, and made a good story of it, at the same time, enjoying Mr. Burrowes' hearty laugh even at his own expense. And Mr. Burrowes, pleased at this proof of confidence, which he knew cost Vindex something, thenceforth promoted George's interests with the utmost cordiality: already understanding that Mr. Newland was prepared to make it worth his while to take him for a partner.

Eleanor's vivid, warm-hearted letters from Italy were delightful. "Picture-letters," Mr. Newland called them; for Mrs. Graydon, finding that they pleased him, often read him the greater part of them. She and Mrs. Debenham got on very well together, but she did not form any other intimate acquaintance.

Miss Clairvaux returned to England at the twelvemonth's end, looking ten years younger. All the dark shadows were gone, and her mind was stored with vivid and cheerful images. Maurice's probation was nearly over, and his historical picture nearly finished, and pronounced at Rome to be a great success. He and Eleanor would soon commence their married life with every prospect of happiness.

"Here is news for you, dear Miss Clairvaux," said Eleanor with the Times supplement in her hand, the morning after their return to Meadowleigh. "Mr. Foljambe is married! 'to Penelope, daughter of Alderman Powis, and widow of Augustus Solms, Esq.'"

"I wish them happy with all my heart," said Miss Clairvaux. "He has too long been a solitary man; unsoftened by family ties. Women can manage to get on without them by making others for themselves; but, 'it is not good for man to be alone.'"

In the course of the morning, Eleanor was

on her way to Stonewall, when she saw a man approaching her, rather remarkable in his dress and gait, though tolerably respectable. When they drew nearer, he proved to be Toby Dick, on his way to the Peaked House. He drew up for a chat, and she spoke to him in a friendly manner. He gave the following account of himself.

"The ewents of the last year have aged me a good deal: I've bid adieu to theatricality. It wore me to see so much wus a clown get all the clapping—a lissom chap enough; but as for his humour!—well, it put me out of humour to hear his weak attempts at it. It's a gift, miss, that is! I don't know how it comes—never know why people laugh at me —but I know why they don't ought to laugh at *him*! That's one thing; and then, that affair of Miss Clairvaux troubled me a good deal. If people like *her* come to grief, why, what do *we* deserve to come to? I don't mean you, you know, but me and the likes of

me. Well, I'm going, therefore, to con-
nubiate; isn't that the gentry's word? Mrs.
Gamage, of the Bunch of Grapes, being be-
widowed, has excepted of me for her next. So
now, you see, I'm going to be a steady man
for life, a re-claimed character, in spite of my
anti-precedents—shall smoke my pipe by my
own fireside, and spell over Bell's Weakly
Mess.—

"One remark I'll make, miss, being now
off the stage—they may talk of their Hamlets,
Othellos, and stuff—it's the fool makes the
farce. The clown is atop of 'em all. Because,
you see, the others have their part to play, and
if it's a poor one, 'taint no fault of theirs. But
he's not a man of parts—his is all extrumpery
genius. But then, if you haven't it, where are
you?

"Well, miss, you'll excuse these poor remarks. We all have our thoughts; only some
can't express them. If you should ever think
it worth while to look in at the Bunch of

Grapes, you know you'll have its master's welcome; but I can't say I expect the pleasure of seeing you."

Here ends the chronicle of Meadowleigh.

THE END.

LONDON:

Printed by A. Schulze, 13, Poland Street.